KILLERS

The Extra Girl

NICOLE M. TAYLOR

E

EPIC Press

The Extra Girl
Killers

Written by Nicole M. Taylor

Published by EPIC Press™
PO Box 398166
Minneapolis, MN 55439

Cover design by Christina Doffing
Images for cover art obtained from iStockPhoto.com
Edited by Jennifer Skogen

LIBRARY OF CONGRESS CATALOGING-IN-PUBLICATION DATA

Names: Taylor, Nicole M., author.
Title: The extra girl / by Nicole M. Taylor.
Description: Minneapolis, MN : EPIC Press, 2017. | Series: Killers
Summary: Struggling starlet Mona McKee attempts to solve the mystery of her seemingly
    miraculous pregnancy then disappears into thin air. Decades later, Mona's personal effects
    fall into blogger Bryce Polk's hands—making him the unlikely investigator in solving the
    secrets of her past.
Identifiers: LCCN 2016946202 | ISBN 9781680764840 (lib. bdg.)
    | ISBN 9781680765403 (ebook)
Subjects: LCSH: Pregnant women—Fiction. | Sisters—Fiction. | Twins—Fiction. |
    Murderers—Fiction. | Murder—Investigation—Fiction. | Missing persons—Fiction. |
    Mystery and detective stories—Fiction. | Young adult fiction.
Classification: DDC [Fic]—dc23
LC record available at http://lccn.loc.gov/2016946202

EPICPRESS.COM

For the Clarionites,
my wise and weird and wonderful
chosen family. Thank you for everything!

1

Starlet

February 4th, 1953. Still winter in most parts of the country, but it was plenty warm in Los Angeles, California where the sun shines all year long. Warm enough that thirty-two-year-old housewife Cherie Platt could take her toddler, Donald Platt, out to the park to play.

In a small gazebo next to a picnic table, young Donald discovered an array of unusual items: a woman's hair comb with long strands of red hair still attached, a small black appointment book with the letter M monogrammed on the cover in gold leaf, and a black pocketbook with a snap-close, empty save for a handful of bobby pins and a receipt for groceries purchased at a nearby supermarket.

With this seemingly simple discovery, Donald and Cherie Platt would unknowingly break one of the most enduring mysteries in LA history.

Locating the owner of the missing items was easy—in addition to the monogram, her name and address were neatly printed on the first page of the appointment book. "Moana McKee," a failed actress and dancer who lived with her mother in a small apartment in LA's Hancock Park neighborhood.

That's when I stopped reading, scrolling down until I found the comments section. I signed in with my real name—Bryce Polk—and included a link to my website because I wanted everyone who read my comment to know that I wasn't just some random troll; I was a goddamned expert.

Wow. This article is so riddled with basic errors that I can't even bring myself to complete it. Here are just a few of the MANY problems I noted:

1. The hair in the comb was not red. Mona McKee

was a strawberry blonde, something that is very apparent if you had bothered to look at even one color photo of her.

2. HER NAME IS NOT MOANA! That name is on the birth certificate, yes, but she went exclusively by Mona for her entire life and that is how she is credited in all of her 62 (yes, *sixty-two*) movies.

Which brings me to . . .

3. Mona McKee was in no way a "failed" actress. (She was also not in any meaningful way "a dancer." She learned choreography for certain roles but she was not trained in any type of dance and would not have considered it her primary specialty.) Over the course of more than a decade, she made more than 50 films and successfully transitioned from child star to serious adult actress—a jump some of today's starlets only WISH they could make. While it is true that she was never a "marquee name" she worked steadily and consistently and had really only begun to come into her own when she vanished.

4. A minor point comparatively but this still goes to show how little you truly understand about this case:

the house (not an apartment as you've stated) was in Mona's name. She purchased it with the money she made in her "failed" acting career. Her mother did reside there, as did her sister and her family, but it was Mona's home.

In the future, please do some basic research before you take it upon yourself to opine about a situation that is still very sensitive to many people.

As soon as I pressed POST I felt a deflation. There was something satisfying about telling off a know-nothing idiot who nevertheless felt comfortable presenting himself as an authority, but it wasn't the sort of thing I was supposed to be doing—not in general and not at that moment. My presentation started in less than fifteen minutes—I'd really just returned to my hotel room to change my shirt and grab my laptop. I had gotten distracted, as usual, by one of my Google alerts for variations on Mona's name.

Some days it seemed that the only people who

still cared about Mona McKee were the ghoulish weirdos who liked to look up old murder stories online. I found her regularly on all sorts of "Most Mysterious Disappearances Ever" and "People Who Just Vanished" lists, in YouTube round-ups of the strangest California mysteries, and on message boards dedicated to dissecting crimes that happened before most of the posters were born.

I wouldn't mind it so much, except that they would invariably fabricate details to spice up what was ultimately a pretty simple and unsatisfying story. Mona was gone and no one knew why but, in their telling, she became a former showgirl, a gangster's moll, a high-end prostitute, and even a Bonnie-and-Clyde-style bank robber. No one ever wanted to talk about her early work in the *Little Sally* series of films or her big break on *At the Sandpiper Inn* or her scene-stealing turn in *Shores of Desire*. No one wanted to speculate about the content of her lost films or extrapolate the direction her career might have taken, had she lived past nineteen.

All they wanted was a good solution to a murder mystery, a cackling perp with blood on his hands.

The sad part was, I would probably get more attention for my website (www.monamckee.com) just from that single pissy comment than I would from this presentation, which I'd spent months preparing (years, if one considered the totality of my scholarship on Mona and other unfairly overlooked "bit players" of the early 1950s). The West Coast Cinema Studies Conference Board had deigned to give me a slot but had made their low opinion of me very clear, putting me at seven p.m. on the first night of the conference. Everyone would either be in the bar or at dinner, still catching up with friends and colleagues and extremely uninterested in a presentation from an unpublished grad student.

As narrow and crappy as the opportunity was, however, it was an opportunity all the same and one that I could not afford to pass up. I still had a fantasy that someone—an enlightened thinker with deep pockets—was going to chance upon me and, seeing the work I was doing, offer to fund my book on Mona. At the very least, presenting at conferences gave me something to point to when my academic advisors demanded to know why my thesis still wasn't finished.

When I got down to the room, however, I knew that today would not be the day that my benefactor appeared. I had been shunted off into one of the smaller rooms with only a folding chair up front—no table—and there were a grand total of three people in the audience. One, an elderly man, was asleep underneath the saggy brim of a bucket hat. The second was a forty-something woman who looked like she might be a member of the hotel's staff or else lost on her way somewhere else, and the last was a young girl scrolling mindlessly through her phone and never once glancing up at me.

Still, they were the only audience I had and what else was I going to do for forty minutes (plus what would undoubtedly be a very unnecessary fifteen-minute Q&A period)? I cleared my throat and started at the beginning—with Mona herself.

. . .

Bryce's Bloggings, June 11th, 2015

What do we grieve for when someone dies young? Or further still: what do we grieve for when someone we've never met, cannot honestly say to have known, is taken before their time? I have no real claim on Mona McKee, who vanished from this earth before my parents were born.

I don't know who took her from that sunny park— or if she was taken at all. I don't know what the mysterious "G.V. knows?" notation in her daybook entry meant (though I do reject the common theory that it referred to marquee heartthrob Gilbert Vale). I don't know why she never returned to the little bungalow she'd purchased free and clear—the first such home anyone in her immediate family had ever owned.

Instead, I know her pictures. Or at least the ones available to me. I know her first appearance as an unsteady toddler in the *Frenike Chicken* short with her voice dubbed in by an adult woman. I know her spectacular turn as Ellen, the plain and timid friend to fearless Little Sally in all fourteen of her adventures. I know the dance number she clearly—yet endearingly—botched in *Mr. Ripper's Wives* and the subtle widening of her eyes when Blake tells Angelene that young Tim is really his son in *Shores of Desire*. I know the part of her hair and her thin, almost reedy singing voice. I know her as a waitress, a mother, a praying woman, a crying child, a dancing adolescent, a hundred permutations of her familiar face. And, I firmly believe, I would have known even more of her, had she lived.

That is what I grieve for when I grieve for Mona McKee; not just one life unlived but hundreds, maybe thousands. If this is what makes Mona's almost certain demise in 1953 more tragic, however, it is also the balm that alleviates some of the pain. In our miserable world, victims are abundant. How many others, though, left such a wealth of documentation behind? We know Mona's every gesture and micro-expression, a full accounting of her life from earliest childhood to just a few months before her passing.

People speak regularly of the magic of film

stars, particularly those stars of what we think of as Hollywood's golden age, but perhaps the only magic is their ability to preserve themselves indefinitely. They crystalize, as if in amber, and no matter how many years pass, when we sit down to watch *Little Sally Learns the Value of a Dollar* or *At the Sandpiper Inn*, our girl is there, ready to laugh and sing and, occasionally, to die. But only until the next viewing.

●　●　●

I was surprised to see that the moment I'd finished my presentation, a hand shot in the air. It was the young girl, who I had half-expected to slip out at some point during the lecture. Instead, she'd sat there the whole time, looking almost constantly at her phone and occasionally tapping out something with her dexterous thumbs.

She was looking at me now, though. Glaring, really. She was very young indeed and half her head was shaved down to fuzz while the other half hung in a smooth, white-blonde bob. She had a ring in her eyebrow, small gauges in her ears and she was wearing loud, plum-colored lipstick. "Yes?" I asked politely.

"Yeah, I just wanted to know, why Mona?"

"Uh . . . I'm not sure what you mean?"

"Why this one person out of the hundreds of other bit players over the years? What's your deal with her?"

I shot a glance at the other members of the audience—the old man was still sleeping but the older woman was watching this exchange with interest. "I found a copy of *Over a Barrel* in undergrad and something about Mona struck me. I've been interested in her ever since."

The character of Laura Caswell in *Over a Barrel* was undoubtedly Mona's most significant role, that of the rebellious daughter of a rich man who wants to shuck her life of privilege and perform as a stunt rider. It was considered a very minor effort in almost all respects: mediocre script, uninspired direction, weak set design, and shoddy acting. Except for Mona. She had clearly poured everything she had into the role and she was, by turns, sulky and spoiled or fearless and untamable. She had a full, unflinching vulnerability, all the more impressive for the general worthlessness of the picture itself. She was just sixteen when filming began.

The young woman narrowed her eyes. "So, you liked a movie? That's it? And you go around posting passive-aggressive blog posts about people and white knighting this chick because of it?"

Ah-ha. So this girl was someone, some blogger whom I had offended with one of my "passive-aggressive blog posts" (which were really just correcting the record to make sure that misinformation was not allowed to stand). "If you do a lot of work on one particular person, you can start to develop something of an attachment to them. A certain protectiveness and, with Mona especially, there are so many people who are only interested in the most superficial aspects of her story."

"So, you're, like, the arbiter of how people get to talk and think about a woman who has been dead for six decades?" she asked with a flat viciousness that made me wonder who she could possibly be to have such a hate-on for me.

"Why don't we take some other questions?" I asked brightly, turning my attention toward the older woman who had a wide-eyed, startled-farm-animal look about her.

"Er . . ." she stuttered, "I just came to listen to the presentation?"

"Any question is okay!" I smiled desperately. "That's what I'm here for!"

The older woman hesitated for a moment but, when I didn't look away from her, asked softly, "In the . . . the book you're doing on her, are you going to talk at all about Mona's going missing?"

I grimaced. "No. I'm a film scholar, not some desperate internet writer trying to create a listicle about LA crime. My interest in Mona McKee is *scholarly*, not prurient, and if that's the sort of content you're looking for, there are plenty of places on the internet to find it. Perhaps she"—I waved my hand dismissively at the younger woman—"could help you out." It was bitter, but I couldn't help it. It wasn't as though someone was paying me to sit there and get attacked by idiots who had no concept of what real scholarship was—what it required.

To my surprise, though, the woman actually seemed . . . relieved? She wasn't angry, at least, and she sat back in her seat, sinking into herself like an abandoned accordion. It didn't seem like she was going to ask another question though and as the only other options were rousing the old guy or going back to that spiteful girl, I decided to just end the presentation early.

"If you want to talk more," I said, "I'll be in the bar."

●　●　●

I ordered three drinks at once to save myself repeat trips then hunkered down in a rounded booth at the back of the bar. I knew that I was supposed to be using this time to network with my peers, but right now, I couldn't muster the fake enthusiasm for their dumb, dull projects, retreads of innumerable other, better works.

Plus, I was invoicing the school for this entire trip and, right now, these $12 gin and tonics were definitely a necessary educational expense.

I was surprised when someone plopped down in the booth next to me and even more surprised to see that it was the older woman from the presentation.

"Connie Leonardo," she said, sticking out her hand.

I took it, nonplussed. "Hi Connie. I'm Bryce."

"Of course," she said, and her eyes flickered toward the glasses arrayed in front of me. "Is this . . . not a good time?"

"Time for what?"

"I have something for you. Something of Mona's."

I squinted at her. She was utterly ordinary looking, like someone's stodgy aunt or the woman failing to return her cart at the grocery store. "You have something that belonged to Mona?"

She hesitated. "Sort of."

I finished my first G&T which did exactly nothing for me. "Ma'am, could you just be straight with me and not waste my time?"

"I have some of Mona's films and I'd like you to see them. I think you have . . . the right sort of eye."

"Gosh, I'm honored." At last, a random midwestern housewife had deemed me competent to look at the films I'd been studying for years. And I had thought I wouldn't get anything out of this conference. "But I have exquisite copies of all of Mona McKee's extant films. I don't need to view yours."

"That's not what I'm talking about," she snapped. "I have other ones. Different ones than what you talk about in your blog. I think some of them are the same as the ones that got lost in that fire down in Culver City."

The 1962 fire in the Culver City Museum of Film had been unquantifiable loss for film history in general and rare film scholarship in particular. Over thirty McKee films were lost in the fire; twenty-four of them had been the sole remaining copies. Mona's films weren't the only casualties, of course, but many of the other films had been digitized or else had duplicates in other collections.

"You're saying you have copies of some of Mona's lost films?"

"Some of them. And some other stuff as well."

"What kind of *stuff?*"

The woman threw up her hands, like I was somehow being unnecessarily difficult. "Just *stuff!* Personal things. Memorabilia, I guess you'd say."

That didn't really interest me. I knew people who obsessively collected bits and pieces of their subjects' lives, I even knew one particularly creepy guy who had purchased a slot in a mausoleum right above the final resting place of a semi-famous actress. He liked to joke about it, saying he'd get on top of her if it killed him. I'd never found it very funny and I'd never felt any need to own Mona's possessions, but it did raise the question of how Connie Leonardo came to have them—if she was telling the truth.

"Do you have proof of any of this?" I asked, starting in on the second drink.

"I have the movies; I brought them with me. You can look at them yourself."

It seemed to come as a surprise that anyone might question her motivations.

"So I'm supposed to just follow you alone to a secondary location in a strange city to 'look at some films'? You know that's how people get their kidneys stolen, don't you?"

"Really?" Connie asked flatly. It was true that she didn't look like a kidney thief but she did look like she might be a big waste of time and I was not a patient person. I shrugged at her and finished my second drink.

"One of them looks like one of those . . . sort of like an audition, I guess? What are those called?" Connie offered, frustration clear in her voice.

"Screen test?"

"Yeah, a screen test for *Lady of Gomorrah*, I think. I recognize the monologue from when Julia Franklin says it in the movie, but I guess Mona went out for it."

Mona had indeed tried out for that picture, as she tried out for almost every ingénue part in 1952—the last full year of her life. She'd written in one of her diaries about how bitterly disappointed she was when she heard they'd decided to go with Franklin instead.

Those diaries were unpublished. They were part of the minuscule rare film library at UC Las Cuevas and I had seen the list of every person who had ever checked them out. Mine was the only name on that list. I wasn't completely convinced that she was telling the truth about having lost films but she must have some source of information about Mona to know about the *Lady of Gomorrah* audition.

"Okay . . . so, why me? There are lots of places that take old films, digitize them or whatever. I study film but I don't do the technical stuff."

Connie shook her head vehemently. "No! That's not what I want. They aren't for public consumption, not yet at least."

Maybe the drinks were stronger than I'd realized because she was making exactly zero sense. "If I look at these films—and they are what you say they are—I'm definitely going to include them in my book. Which will be available to the public." Technically available. It would be archived in the university's library among the thousands of other theses that grad students had completed over the years, destined to do nothing more exciting than maybe grow some mold.

She waved one careless hand. "That's fine, that's great. I think these films should be studied. It doesn't feel right, just leaving them all boxed up. I just don't want . . . any problems for my family."

I glared down at the second glass, which had the temerity to be empty of everything except a slice of lime. "Why would old movies cause your family problems?"

"I've approached some other people about this," Connie said, not really answering my question, "but they weren't really interested in Mona as an actress. They just wanted to know all about the . . . the mystery of it. But you're not like that. That's why I came all the way here to see you, so I could be sure. If you don't take them now, I think I'll probably have to destroy them."

"Wait, wait, wait," I said, reaching out for her arm. "Let's not jump any guns. I'll look at the films, okay? But if there's something about all this, something you don't want me to include in the book, you have to tell me."

Connie pursed her lips so tightly it seemed painful and looked around the bar. We were practically alone, buried there in the back, and everyone else was engaged in loud, animated conversations in small groups. No one was listening, no one cared. Story of my professional life.

"I'm pretty sure," Connie said finally, in a low and genuinely anxious voice, "that my Granddad killed Mona McKee."

2

Ends Meet

It was a whodunnit and Mona was "it." She was playing the daughter of a judge or a senator, some sort of muckity-muck. She only appeared on camera twice (once in a photograph, once in a coffin) so they hadn't even bothered sending her script pages.

For the coffin scene, the director didn't give her anything to work with. She supposed he figured that she knew how to play dead. After all, even dogs could do that. When her scene was over, she bummed a cig off Gene, who wasn't a writer on the picture but was hanging around anyway. "I'm so tired of these lousy one-day gigs," she sighed, a plume of smoke exiting her mouth along with the words.

"It'll turn around," Gene assured her. "You're a star on the rise."

She squinted at him. "Can you really be a star on the rise when you've been in the game for eleven years?"

"I always forget about those old Sally movies," he laughed. "I don't know if that really counts." But Mona was sure it did. She might be "on the rise" but she had lost her chance, she knew, to be a precocious breakout star.

She took another drag on her cigarette, which was doing nothing for the pounding in her head. She'd woken up this morning with a feeling as though someone had cleft her skull in two, but she didn't dare miss her "big" day of filming. The headaches were practically a regular thing now, anyway. Three or four times a week she'd wake up with a dull, thumping pain in her skull, a thick, sore throat, and aching in her limbs. It was like a cold that never fully bloomed but never really went away either.

Across the lot, there was the sound of scuffling and shouting as though men were at work. Both Mona and Gene looked up to see a group of people moving from one studio to another. It was an odd sort of parade with writers, assistants, and assorted errand-boys and hangers-on all trying to move in a great cluster while each individual person struggled to get closer to the figure at the center of the crowd: a hunched man with a newspaper inexplicably stretched over his head.

"What's all that commotion?"

Gene chuckled. "Prince Charming himself. He's been shooting for a couple of days now."

Mona's eyebrows shot up. "Gideon Vale? I had no idea." Imagine that! Here she was, working on the same lot with Gideon Vale.

"They're keeping it pretty quiet. Apparently it's just about impossible to keep the set clean when the press finds out he's working."

Gene would know these things; he had been an assistant writer on one of Gideon's pictures with Lydia Leighton. It was the kind of thing that might have been a big break for someone but Gene hadn't seemed to make much of it.

"What's he doing?"

"Song and dance thing, from what I hear."

"Really? After the last one?"

"Apparently he's determined to make it work."

Just another example of Gideon Vale's legendary stubbornness. Or his equally legendary vanity. His first foray into musicals—a sea-faring farce called *Captain Redbeard*—had massively under-performed (well, for a Vale film, which still put it several leagues ahead of anything Mona had ever been in). Worse, however, was the critical savaging he'd gotten in the press. The consensus was that he just wasn't built for hoofing, nor for singing, and that he was best served going back to the kind of leading-man roles that had made him famous.

He could have done just that—made another

string of movies with Lydia Leighton or Molly Francis and kept everyone happy, but Mona guessed that Vale couldn't tolerate a failure, no matter how seemingly minor. It bothered her more and more as the years wore on, how some people got so much, so many chances, and how others had to make do with crumbs. What she wouldn't give for a chance to toe the line for a major studio!

"You got the time, Gene?" she asked, flicking her cigarette away. He turned his watch toward her and Mona sighed. The damn director could keep her here all day on the off-chance he needed another shot of her not doing anything but she was supposed to hit The Paper Lantern by nine-thirty for a gig. It wasn't anything to brag about. In fact, her mother would have said it was "next door to being a hoochie-coochie girl" but the pay was good, which was more than she could say for a job like this that ate up her whole day and offered little more than scale in return.

They probably wouldn't need her again today

but, if she left and the director did summon her and find her gone, that was the kind of black mark it would take her months or years to get over. If you couldn't be famous, you had to be a professional.

So Mona waited, her belly grumbling insistently. She never ate on shooting days to avoid bloating on camera. Today, though, she was feeling the hunger more keenly than usual. She gestured for Gene to give over another cigarette—something small and simple to cut the pain.

.　.　.

She was forty minutes late to the club and the manager looked like he wanted to break her in half. Luckily for Mona, she was the biggest deal on that stage. No one else up there had done anything higher profile than a girly show in Vegas.

She barely had time to squeeze into her costume before the manager practically kicked her out onto the stage. Apparently one of the waitresses, a hard-done-by brunette named Misty, had been standing in for her. Mona could see the audience sizing her up quizzically when she emerged from the wings. Her sister Rita, who had insisted upon coming and bringing her husband Clark along, was seated at a table stage right. She looked at Mona with a haughty sort of disapproval.

Rita still wouldn't watch the lion's share of Mona's films but she refused to stay away from this performance at a shabby little nightclub. She only wanted to watch when she could see Mona fail.

The show was a little musical farce, a loose collection of sketches with a few songs interspersed. Mona was a far better comedienne than she was a singer but, at the end of the day, it was really about how her legs looked in her stockings. And they looked good.

But how much longer could she count on that? Mona woke up each morning with a faint terror lying over her, like a thin sheet in the summer time. She worried she had lost it, somehow, in the middle of the night. That *this* was the morning she would wake up and find that her skin was no longer bright and warm, her face no longer symmetrical, her hair no longer lustrous and gold, her body less lean, her breasts less high.

She examined herself from all angles in the bathroom she shared with Rita, Rita's husband, and the girls' mother Ramona. She charted the size and color of the dark puffs of skin under her eyes, the depth of the little lines at the corners of her smile and between her eyebrows. She examined the freckles and spots on her chest and shoulders, she looked appraisingly at the flat plane of her stomach, vanishing inevitably into the right angles of her hip bones. She pulled the sides of her thighs tight until even the flecks and dimples of fat under the skin vanished. She lifted her head and turned her chin to endless angles, searching ever for the one that hid all her flaws and highlighted all her virtues.

All of that happened in the tiled confines of the bathroom, however. When she stepped out into the world, Mona tried to be steady and certain in her body. First and foremost, she must believe in her own incandescence, her own transcendent beauty and perpetual youth. So armed, she could fool the world.

●   ●   ●

After the show, the manager paid her, minus ten percent "because she was late." Mona thought about arguing him back to their agreed-upon rate but, at some point during the show, both Rita and Clark had vanished and she needed to track them down. She certainly didn't want Rita to catch her begging some sleaze for a couple extra bucks.

"And get your goddamned sister, she's been locked in the bathroom for fifteen minutes," the manager grumped, folding up the paper enveloped he'd paid her out of and tucking it in his breast pocket. Mona had a fantasy—fleeting and stupid—of getting up close to him and sneaking her hand into that pocket.

Instead, she just made her way to the back of the bar, through the ill-lit hallway to the ladies' room, which Clark had pressed himself up against. He was thumping his forehead rhythmically against the door. "Come out, come out, come out," he kept saying, until it was more like a moan of pain than human words. "You know how I am. You *know*," he insisted.

Mona reached past him hesitantly and rapped the door with her knuckles. "Show's over," she called out. "Time to go home."

There was a distant rustling behind the door before it swung open, revealing Rita, her face red and glossy, as though she had been crying or perhaps sweating. She swept past Clark and took Mona's hand, pulling her along with her. Mona hadn't even changed out of her costume but she allowed Rita to drag her out of the club. She could always pick her things up later and she knew better than to argue with Rita when she was in a lather.

When they got outside the bar, Rita took a deep breath—nearly a gasp, in fact—as though she were surfacing after a long underwater dive. "That show is indecent," she said, almost immediately. "You know Mother would never have approved that if she were in her right mind."

Rita ushered them down Sunset toward the bus stop and Mona struggled to keep up, extra-tall heels keeping her unbalanced. "The pay is good," Mona said, extremely thankful that Rita had locked herself in the bathroom while the manager stiffed Mona.

"The grocery store is hiring," Rita informed her. "A dollar twenty-five an hour. They need checkers and baggers. I could put in a word for you with the manager. You could get started as quick as next week."

Mona snorted. "That's ridiculous. A single good part would blow your dollar twenty-five right out of the water."

"And was this a good part? Flashing your private parts for a bunch of leering goons?"

"Like your husband?" Mona shot back. She wondered if that was what they were fighting about, if Clark had been just a little too attentive to the show. Not that the two of them needed a reason to go at it. They'd been married just under six months and almost every other night ended with Clark hitting the walls, himself, or Rita. During their brief courtship, he had a good job working on a dairy farm up north, but he'd been laid off shortly after the wedding and his constant malingering around the house hadn't done much for the marriage.

Rita stopped right there in the middle of the sidewalk and dealt Mona a vicious slap. It was the sort of thing she never would have dared to do before their mother got sick. Or even before Mona's career started to flounder. The one golden rule in the McKee house was that no one upset the golden goose, but these days, Mona was being treated more like a tin-plated duck. "You don't understand anything about my marriage," Rita hissed, which was certainly true. Mona didn't understand why someone as fierce as Rita would try so hard to hold on to a jobless bum who hit her where the bruises wouldn't show if she dared to stay out past nine p.m. or forgot to bring oranges home from the grocery store.

Rita had such a sureness in herself. Mona knew that her sister did not spend the morning inspecting her body for new flaws. She did not transform in her mind each bite of pie or pork roast into dimpled thighs and wobbling arms. She did not care if her waist or her legs were thick, so long as they were good and useful. Rita rarely looked in mirrors at all because she always knew exactly what she would see.

And still she let a worthless two-bit bully like Clark boss her around.

"And you don't seem to understand that my *indecent* job is keeping this family afloat," Mona told her sister frostily. "Besides, I am booking real work too. I have a great part in a detective picture right now, in fact. I'm the most important part." It wasn't technically a lie. The dead body *was* the most important part of any murder mystery.

* * *

When they got home, their mother called Mona into the sitting room, which had long since been converted into a convalescent room for the older woman. "Did you do good tonight, baby?" she asked fondly, and Mona stretched herself out on her mother's legs (when had they become so brittle and so thin, like two broomsticks stuck in a house dress?).

Her mother smoothed Mona's hair reflexively, staring at nothing in particular on the fuzzing television set. Mona could recall many a night like this, her mother dispensing comfort and affection, though only after her performance was finished successfully.

Clark stomped in about a half hour after them

and he barely spared a glance for Mona before he went to the small bedroom he shared with Rita. Almost immediately, the sound of their raised voices floated outward to fill the house.

"I'm gonna get dinner, Momma," Mona said, rising from the sofa-bed and heading for the kitchen where she thought there was some cold chicken left in the ice box. When she opened the refrigerator, however, the deprivations of the day overtook her. She ate the remaining cold chicken and a container of mashed potatoes as well, along with a peanut butter and jelly sandwich and a glass of milk to finish. Her mother watched placidly from the sofa and Mona couldn't help but imagine the look of horror and scorn Mother would have worn if she saw Mona eating like that back when she was altogether in her mind.

Mona staggered then toward the bathroom, moving slow and heavy like a drunk. She had that familiar antsy, overfull feeling she got whenever she ate too much. A desperate urge to get it out of her, at any cost. *Too much, too much,* it seemed to pulse through her blood like something lower and more elemental than a thought.

The bathroom shared a wall with Rita and Clark's room. Occasionally, the mirror rattled in its supports when the wall shook. It sounded like someone was being slammed repeatedly against the opposite side of the wall.

Mona lodged the scale against the door, for it had no lock. She worked quickly, wetting her fingers with her tongue before applying them to the back of her throat and bringing up all her hastily devoured dinner.

There it was—chicken, potatoes, peanut butter, and bread all in a milky slurry. When she had first started performing this ritual as a young girl, she had done it for very practical reasons—there were few better ways to eliminate excess food from her body and Mona had never been very good at denying herself for too long. Now, though, after years of sustained efforts, it almost hurt not to do it. If she didn't void herself, she wouldn't be able to sleep, instead imagining the slow breakdown of all the foodstuffs she'd eaten, how they traveled to every part of her body and weighed her down.

When she was done, Mona brushed her teeth over the sink. She looked pale underneath her show makeup and the swollen skin under her eyes was a dull blueish purple. She looked weak and deflated but also hollow, which was the best she could hope for.

It had been a while since she had to purge. Maybe it was the long, pointless hours on the shoot today, or the humiliation over the lost ten percent. Or Rita's scolding. Mona put her hands on her hips and pouched her stomach slightly, still distended from her recent gluttony. Perhaps it was her monthlies, which Mona thought should be approaching soon.

Mona spit toothpaste bubbles into the sink and washed them away immediately. As she did so, the mirror shook again, causing her reflection to waver.

She heard a short scream and recognized her sister's voice. There was a deep rumble then and silence. Mona hoped that meant it was over for the evening.

Back when they first moved in, Mona had tried to intervene once but Rita herself had nearly pulled out Mona's hair dragging her out of the room. "Never," Rita said to her, furious, "get between me and my husband."

And so Mona let it be, the shouts and the thumps and the bruises in the morning. *Don't we all have our problems?* she thought, leaning over to flush.

3

Ingenue

I swallowed my last G&T in two painful gulps, eager to get up from the table and away from this looney. I should have known this would happen eventually. I'd had plenty of people write me online to tell me all about how their dad or uncle or grandpa killed Mona in between cutting up the Black Dahlia and being the Zodiac Killer (somehow the Zodiac Killer always snuck in there).

"I'm not going to plug your book or write a post about your theory or link your website or whatever you think you're gonna get out of this interaction, okay?" I said, partially standing up. Connie was blocking the way out of the booth, however. Unless I wanted to do a very undignified crab-crawl over her, I had nowhere to go.

"I don't have a website or a book, none of that," she said.

I sat back down because I started to feel stupid, up on my feet and going nowhere. "Look, I have talked to a lot of people who believe that someone they know was responsible for Mona's disappearance. I'm not saying they're crazy. I'm not even saying they're wrong. I'm just saying, it's not my job to figure out what happened to her."

"Yes!" Connie burst out in frustration. "That's all I want, for you to watch the movies and write your book or whatever and just . . . put it out there. Like she would have wanted."

What Mona McKee would have wanted, I thought, was to live past nineteen and to have the kind of career she deserved.

"So . . . you're telling me that you'll let me view all

these rare, lost films and all I have to do in exchange is not publicly call your grandfather a murderer?"

Connie gave me an exasperated nod. "I feel like it's the least we can do, after . . ."

"After your grandpa killed her?" I supplied and earned myself a sharp glare.

"I don't appreciate your tone," she said. "I'm trying to do the right thing here."

Sure, the "right" thing to do upon discovering that a family member had murdered another human being was to help a Ph.D. student to write a book about that person's filmography. Honestly, though, I was just so damn curious about the whole thing at that point that I felt like I had to take a look at her "films" if only to see what exactly she thought was so important that she had to do all this cloak and dagger crap to keep it a secret.

"Okay," I said. "I won't mention your family's name. Show me what you've got."

. . .

I must have been seriously drunk because I didn't even notice the girl following me up to my room until she reached out and tugged on the sleeve of my blazer. "You gotta let me see those films," she hissed—her version of a whisper, I supposed.

It was the girl from the presentation, face illuminated by the glow of her ever-present cell phone.

"What . . . the fuck?" I sputtered, stumbling back into my unopened hotel room door. My key fluttered out of my hands and the girl crouched down to retrieve it.

"Here," she said cheerfully. "When is she bringing the films? Is it tonight?" She looked from me to the key in my hand with expectation.

"What are you talking about?"

"That woman with the films. Mona's lost films, I want to see them."

Had she been listening in to my conversation with Connie at the bar? I hadn't seen her, but it was a dark corner. Was she crouched there, hiding?

I tried to size her up, wondering if, like Connie,

she had come to this conference specifically for me. She had certainly seemed to have a beef with me in the presentation. She was petite, significantly shorter than me, and a little thick. Still, I doubted she could overpower me in a fight, if that was what she was after. Unless she'd brought a weapon.

"Are you *stalking* me?"

She gave me a tremendous eye-roll. "I was going to *talk* to you, like you said after the presentation."

"That was not a sincere offer—"

"But that woman was there and I heard what she was saying and I want in."

"There's nothing to be *in* on," I said. "She may not even have anything."

"But if she does—"

"If she does, it's none of your business. I'm the pre-eminent scholar on McKee's work and I'm the person Ms. Leonardo approached. If she wanted a random teenager to see the films, she would have asked you."

"I'll scoop you." The girl held out her cell phone,

opened to what looked like Tumblr page crowded with words. "I already did a full write up of everything I heard and, if you don't let me see the films, I'll make their existence public and draw down anyone who gives even the mildest of shits about lost films. Or unsolved murder cases."

She grinned at me, her purple lips looking odd and inhuman in the reflected phone light.

"No one cares about your little Tumblr." I tried to sound as imperious as possible but we both knew she'd found a weak point. Lure in the unsolved crime weirdos and people would be beating a path to Connie Leonardo's door. It was exactly what Connie didn't want and it would probably mean I'd never see anything she had—if she had anything at all.

The girl snorted. "I average three thousand hits a year. What does monamckee.com do? Five hundred?"

It was actually more like three hundred, many of them spam bots that posted impenetrable comments in Russian, and several were the result of tortured search terms like "hollywood MILF in the park redhead."

"And what are you going to do if I let you view the films?"

"I'm going to write about them," she said, as though that should have been obvious. "I'm a film scholar, after all."

"What are you, seventeen?" I laughed.

She colored slightly. "Eighteen. But there's no age limit on scholarship. Look at yourself, you're like twenty-five."

"Twenty-one," I corrected automatically and she gave me a surprised look. "I was a smart kid."

"A smart kid? You must have gone to college when you were like—"

"Fifteen. Yeah."

"So you were like some child prodigy?" she asked, sly and a little mocking. "That explains your lack of social development."

"I wasn't a child prodigy," I sighed. There are two kinds of "prodigies": the rare and genuine geniuses who were significantly advanced compared to their peers and would continue to outstrip them for the rest of their lives, and those who, in their youth, experienced a brief period of accelerated development but eventually stalled out and remained stagnant until their cohort caught up with them. I had been—was—the latter. "And we aren't talking about me. I don't even know your name."

A few expressions flickered across her face: surprise, pique, and then a certain arch meanness which remained as she stuck out her hand for shaking. "I'm Flavia Cutler," she said. "Or, as you may know me, a vapid, intellectually-empty fashion blogger who should stay in her lane before she entirely embarrasses herself."

Oh shit.

•   •   •

I had actually "met" Flavia about six months previously when she'd done a short feature on Mona for her "vintage film" website. She'd analyzed some screenshots from *Shores of Desire* in a rudimentary way, focused almost entirely on the costuming but with a few comments about Mona's body language and her use of space. I'd written what I thought was a very even-handed critique.

Evidentially, Flavia did not feel the same.

She never responded to me, neither privately nor on her website, but she began featuring Mona's films much more prominently after that, even somehow managing to find copies of the rarer late-period movies. Her analysis was still lacking and she'd never even mentioned my name, though my work had clearly informed hers.

I thought that was a pretty shabby way to treat someone who had gone out of his way to help her and who had clearly sparked a new interest for her, but apparently it was Flavia who somehow felt she was the wronged party.

"I assumed you'd recognized me," she said, after

I had finally opened the door and ushered her inside my room. "My picture is online."

Another sure sign that the content was lacking. Who cared what the writer looked like? "I'm not a very visual person," I said, crouching down to peer inside the stocked mini-fridge. Seventeen dollars for a flask-sized bottle of mid-range vodka? Jesus.

"So you went into film studies, naturally," Flavia said.

"Film is different," I told her. It wasn't about the pure visuals—though that was obviously part of it—it was a full sensory experience and something deeper as well, something that tapped into the buried lizard brain. I sometimes felt that the only time I could experience the full range of human emotions was when I was parked in front of a shimmering screen. "Did you seriously come all this way just to hassle me?" I took my own phone out of my pocket, waiting for Connie's text. She said she had to get "the stuff" from her car. This whole thing had a certain drug deal vibe to it. Not that I would know what a drug deal felt like.

"Of course not. I came here because I'm studying cinema, just like you."

"Oh, okay." I hadn't exactly meant it to sound sarcastic but that was kind of my default tone.

"You're a real superior douchebag, you know that?" Flavia stalked restlessly around the room, uncomfortable, apparently, with the idea of sitting down anywhere.

"I'm just saying that liking fifties fashion and watching a bunch of movies because somebody online hurt your delicate feelings doesn't make you a serious student of cinema."

Finally, she sat down, pulling the chair away from the desk to face me. "Is that what you think I've been doing? Analyzing Mona's films to, like, get back at you or something?"

I sipped my watery vodka. "The timing is convenient."

"Sure, your shitty little post about me might

have made me take a closer look at her films, but I I like Mona. A Hapa girl trying to make it in 1950s Hollywood? That's awesome and she was awesome and no one knows. She's like this undiscovered gem; she could be the Anna May Wong of Pacific Islanders."

"Except that there's no proof she was . . . what did you call it?"

"Hapa. Dude, her birth name was Moana. You can't tell me there wasn't some Hawaiian up in there. Plus, changing your name so you don't weird out the white folks is, like, one of the most Asian things you can do."

"I don't know how I feel about you making her your . . . personal racial mascot. Are you Hapa?" I peered at her. Her hair was blonde but that was clearly a dye job, and her skin was medium-brown. Her eyes were startlingly dark, almost black, really.

"Me? Oh, I'm one part none of your business and two parts go fuck yourself."

"Jesus, forget I asked," I mumbled into my plastic cup.

"Oh, I won't," Flavia said cheerfully. "But, I gotta say, for someone who is so concerned with Mona not being a 'racial mascot,' you are awfully invested in Mona's whiteness."

"I'm a scholar. I'm invested in the truth."

"And Mona was an actress," Flavia pointed out. "It was her job to pretend to be what she wasn't."

• • •

Connie was predictably alarmed when she got to my room and discovered I was not alone. "This is Flavia, my . . . research assistant." It was hard to get the words out but I couldn't think of any other explanation that would put her at ease.

"I didn't know you had a research assistant," Connie said, regarding Flavia suspiciously. Still, she allowed me to usher her into the room, heavily laden with a couple of canvas shopping bags and what appeared to be an old-fashioned suitcase.

She set the suitcase and one of the canvas sacks

down but held the other in a two-handed death grip. "My mother had them converted to video in the eighties so my grandma could see them. They only ever watched the footage once, I think. It was . . . difficult for my grandmother. The originals are still in the house in Reseda."

"What exactly is on these tapes that was so upsetting for your grandma?" Flavia asked, craning her neck forward in a transparent attempt to see inside the bag Connie was studiously holding closed.

"It's not like a snuff film or anything," Connie said. "It's just . . . well, you'll know what I mean when you see it but it's very clear from these movies that Granddad was hung up on Mona McKee."

"Lots of men at that time probably were," I pointed out, as gently as I could. "She was a very beautiful young woman and screen stars have always attracted ardent admirers."

"Granddad wasn't an audience member. He knew Mona. Personally." Connie looked down at the bag in her hands as though musing upon exactly how "personal" their relationship had been. "He was a writer in Hollywood when he was a young man and he worked with Mona on a few different films. This footage is from all over. Some of this is actually from the films and some of it looks like . . . outtakes, I guess you'd say? People messing up or stuff falling over. And there's some stuff that he shot himself." Connie shifted, uncomfortable. "The one constant is Mona. She's the only person or thing who appears in all the footage. And Granddad kept it, locked up in the attic until he died."

"That's . . . "

"Super creepy?" Flavia supplied.

"I was going to say a little strange, but sure, it's creepy. But it doesn't prove or even really suggest that he had anything to do with Mona going missing," I pointed out.

"Except it's not just the movies." Connie nudged the suitcase with her toe. "He kept this with the reels and I'm pretty sure it's Mona's stuff. There's clothes in there that wouldn't have fit Grandma and all these weird . . . writings. Letters or notes or whatever, they don't make any sense to me."

Now that was interesting. Mona kept scrupulous diaries throughout her short life and she always encoded them with a basic substitution cipher (which I had been the first to crack back when I was completing my master's) but I had never been able to find the diary that covered the last four months of her life. Either she had abruptly ceased her lifetime habit of recording each day or the diary had been hidden— possibly destroyed. Perhaps it had been in Connie's attic all this time?

Flavia was looking at the suitcase with undisguised greed though probably for wholly unrelated reasons. She was undoubtedly imagining all the vintage "treasures" contained within.

"I brought a VCR," Connie offered, lifting the second canvas bag. "I know the hotels don't really have them anymore."

"Would you like to view the films with us?" I asked. I knew that professional decorum probably demanded that I wait and take the material back home with me but I also knew that there was no way in hell I was going to sit on the films all weekend without at least checking to ensure their authenticity.

Connie gave a tight little shake of her head. "I don't really like to watch them. Something . . . feels wrong about it."

"I understand," I said, though I didn't really. Connie had clearly let some sort of weird superstition or mental block develop around these films. It wasn't as though Mona's unquiet ghost would stand over her disapprovingly if she watched them.

"This one," Connie reached into the back and selected a videotape in a nubbly black plastic case, "is the most complete. I don't think the movie ever got made, that's probably why."

She held it out and, for a second, it looked like Flavia was going to go for it. Like there was any way I'd let her have the first look. I snatched it up, opening the case to find an unlabeled tape. "It's something about a boarding school, I think. Mona's not in it much," Connie said.

"Wait a minute—is this *The Redfield House?*"

The Redfield House was a famously unfinished film in production around the time of Mona's death. It was a *Daddy Long Legs*-style school story about a widowed professor who finds new life teaching philosophy at a girl's school. And, of course, he falls in love with one of the older seniors (played by Lydia Leighton, who would have been a very unconvincing teenager at that point in her career if you asked me). There had been rumors that Mona was in the movie, but I'd never been able to substantiate them.

It was a contract-fulfillment picture for Gideon Vale, who naturally played the male lead. He'd agreed to it only to force the studio to fund his attempt at another musical and, allegedly, he was resentful of the project from the beginning. Rumor had it that, at some point, he just refused to do any further scenes, utterly crippling the film. The studio eventually chose to shutter the project rather than alienate their cash cow.

Even if Mona didn't appear in a single frame, it would be an invaluable piece of film history. I glanced at Flavia to see if she had any idea how significant this was but she was fiddling with the suitcase, trying to get the lock open. For all her alleged interest in Mona as an actress, it was the clothes she really cared about.

Connie kindly helped me hook the VCR to the hotel's TV and, for someone who was so hesitant to show these tapes to me, she seemed oddly comfortable leaving them with us. She seemed almost relieved, in fact, and I had to stop her at the door and ask if she wanted me to send her my thoughts after I'd reviewed the material.

"It'll be in the book, right?" Connie looked startled. "I'll . . . uh . . . I'll read it there." Her eyes moved toward Flavia and the opened suitcase and there was something weird in her expression, something uneasy and almost pitying. Something guilty.

4

A Delicate Condition

Mona had been forced to develop a code for her diaries early on. If she didn't, Rita was sure to read them and use all the information they contained to her advantage.

In addition to the letter code, she used a series of symbols to mark important occasions. One was a tiny blooming rose, which she used to mark the first day of her menses. Usually, those roses appeared as reliably as the sunrise, leafing back through her entries, Mona realized that the last rose was more than seven weeks before.

Seven weeks. Mona had never been that late in her

life, not even that first year when she was still a kid. She'd known other women who quit cycling when they reduced too much. It came with a set of other symptoms though, like the soft, light hair that grew on their stick-thin arms or the jutting of each bone in their wrists. Mona wasn't like that. If anything, she was bloating, her midsection was soft with what she thought of as "extra," and her cheeks were fuller, though she thought that might be a result of purging too much—it made her throat and face all swollen.

The only other sickness that Mona knew would make a woman stop bleeding was the nine-month sickness that every up-and-coming actress knew to avoid at all costs. It was true that she was hungry and seemed to get tired so much easier these days and she had noticed that her sense of smell had become strangely acute. She could smell the acrid scent of urine even down the hall from the bathroom in her own room and she'd thrown out three perfectly good (or so Rita said) apples because they smelled like rot to her. She didn't know if that was something that happened when woman got with child but it didn't seem like a symptom of anything else either.

But as many questions as pregnancy would answer, it created even more. Mainly because Mona had never been with a man before. Her Momma worked hard to make sure that Mona was always above reproach.

Mona built her career around her body (and her face, of course); it was her instrument and her primary tool for making money and she was content to manipulate it into all sorts of characters and situations. But still she couldn't cotton the idea of showing her body to someone in person without any of the barriers or protections she habitually wore. In person, in the ever-unflattering light of the real world, how would she appear to someone else? Would they notice the outward bow of her lower stomach? The soft flesh at the top of her thighs, as pale and wobbly as a poached egg? She could clearly picture the creeping disappointment on this imagined man's face and how hard he would try to hide it.

If it was not a child, perhaps it was something

even worse, some kind of sickness or wrongness down there? There was her mother, after all, and that kind of problem ran in families . . . She couldn't afford something like that right now, not when she was working two or three gigs at a time to keep up with the payments on the house.

Maybe it was just a fluke, a little trick her body was playing on her? Maybe, if she just gave it some time, it would go away.

• • •

Momma was dying. Everyone in the house skirted around that fact like it was an old and cumbersome piece of furniture—too heavy to be moved, too ugly to contemplate. The doctor told them she had a tumor in her brain. They'd have to chop up her brain if they wanted to take it out. She'd never survive the operation and, if she did, she'd have no speech, no memory, no nothing.

Instead, the doctor prescribed something for the

pain, though Momma never complained. In many ways, the last few months might have been the happiest time in her mother's life. Ever since Mona could remember, her mother had been in one kind of pain or another. Her back was curved from years of crouching on a stool in a factory during the war. Her heart was broken from years of wear and disappointment with the two girls God had allotted her. Her feet were sore, her head was heavy, her stomach ached, and all the time, she felt a hurt that she could not name or ascribe to any particular body part. That's how it used to be.

The doctor told the sisters that the tumor was pressing on part of Momma's brain and changing how she thought, even who she was. All Mona knew was that, for the first time, her mother was free from pain.

Mona ate her meals with her mother, sitting on the end of the sofa bed. It was better than waiting for Rita and Clark, who passed each meal in smoldering silence with the occasional eruption into violence.

"I'm working on a new picture," Mona told her mother conversationally. "We have wardrobe fittings today." Mona was a little worried about that in fact, though she didn't dare tell her mother. She remembered very well how her mother used to make her do calisthenic exercises through the night when her wardrobe had been too small or ill-fitting. Mona had been tall for her age and she developed early. Toward the end of the *Little Sally* series, she no longer looked appropriate in the pert little dresses they wanted her to wear and she'd felt the full brunt of her mother's frustration over that fact.

"I'm practically an extra," she said, "but the studio is being pretty good to us." It was a half-truth at best. Mona knew that if she didn't fit into her costume, she would either have to trade with one of the others or else she'd be off the picture. All over a few inches of fabric. An extra was a step above set dressing (and, frequently, not even that). Replacing her would be like trading one rug for another, or deciding to go with a different vase in one scene.

She was eight weeks late now, and every night she prayed that she would wake up and find blood between her legs. She wasn't sure if she was imagining it or not, but it seemed too that her body was getting bigger, if only in increments. Her bust seemed slightly swollen and her stomach as well but, when she got out her measuring tape, she was still at the same numbers she had recorded the previous week.

To look at her mother, a person might not know she was anything other than a slightly frail older woman. There was no bulbous swelling on her head, no glazed look in her eyes or horrible sores. She was going to die, sooner rather than later, and it was all happening inside her skull, beneath the hair that Mona brushed for her every night before going to sleep.

Every morning, when she woke up and found not even the smallest traces of red, Mona thought about that. About how a cancer can grow in the dark, how it can kill you without ever once really showing itself.

But then the day began and she always had

something else to do, somewhere to hurry off to. She had a good gig now and she wasn't going to ruin it with all her petty fears.

Her mother gave her a dry-lipped kiss on the forehead before she left. "Beautiful girl," she called her. It was something she used to say when Mona was very, very young, but she hadn't said it in years. Until she got sick. "Good luck," she said, which was also something she wouldn't have told Mona before. Luck, her mother always said, was for people who could afford it. The rest of the world had to work.

* * *

Nobody wanted the socialite on the lot. She was a mediocre actress and pretty enough in person, but not such hot stuff on the camera. More importantly, though, she just lacked experience. She was always getting in someone's way or blocking someone's shot or screwing up her eyeliner. Mona might have taken pity on her, except that she showed up half the time in clothes and makeup that had been slept in, smelling like cigarette and reefer smoke both.

She was a strange exception to the typical rule that a person either had to be a huge moneymaker or consummate professional to get by in pictures. Instead, she was independently wealthy and connected. She had allegedly lobbied hard for her relatively ignoble role as an extra.

Word around set was that she thought film was the thing for her. She was going to be a star and not just in a certain circle. If that was really so, Mona thought, then she might want to work just a little bit harder. Of course, she was born into the kind of money Mona only dreamed about—hard work had probably never been a big part of her life.

Mona hadn't really had much to do with her until they found themselves in the bathroom for the same purpose. The socialite had no shame, or else hadn't had time to pause and close the bathroom stall door before she began vomiting. Mona at least managed to enclose herself in the next stall before her small breakfast came up. For once, she'd done nothing to induce this. She'd been sitting with other gals, waiting to be called forward, when she began to sweat uncomfortably, though the room was temperate enough. She felt a swirling nausea in her stomach—not the stretched feeling she had before deliberately purging but the low, sickly feeling she got when she had the flu or something similar.

When Mona staggered out of the stall, feeling as though she had been rapidly turned inside-out, the socialite was standing at the wash basin lifting a cupped hand full of water to her mouth. She swished the water between her teeth then spit it back into the white sink, giving Mona a wry look. "You tie one on as well, cutie?"

Mona shook her head mutely and stepped to the next sink, small clutch purse in hand. She kept a toothbrush in there for obvious reasons. The socialite watched her thoughtfully while she brushed her teeth, hair clamped in one hand to keep it out of the sink.

"What?" Mona said, spitting.

"Are you . . . feeling okay?"

Mona rolled her eyes. "I wouldn't be tossing my cookies if I was feeling fine and fancy-free."

"You're just looking . . . well, bad, I guess is how I would put it."

Mona turned to look at the woman full-on. She was petite. So petite in fact that she probably shouldn't have been cast as one of the girls' school extras, who had been selected for their uniform height and size. But she had a scrappiness about her, a toughness that made her seem older than Mona imagined she probably was.

"I'm no good time girl," Mona said stiffly and, to her surprise, the little woman laughed. Mona had expected her to be offended.

"Of course you ain't," she grinned. "You would be working a better class of gigs if you were." She turned back to the mirror like she was expecting Mona to just leave.

"What . . . what do you mean by that?" Mona

asked instead. Without really thinking about it, she had crossed her arms over her lower stomach.

"Look around." She dabbed a fresh coat of lipstick on her parted lips. "You're not homely and you've got a good shape. You're talented and you work hard but you're still taking thankless background work. That's the mark of a good girl. Or one who ain't so good at being bad."

Mona might have been a virgin but she was no sheltered hothouse flower. She knew the kinds of things some girls did to get ahead. But her mother had always assured her she didn't need that.

The socialite finished up her work and hooked her own purse over her shoulder. She paused to look at Mona and gave her a surprisingly kind smile, her lips now crimson and shining. Mona thought the makeup woman would make her wipe that off before she got back on set. All the extra girls had a uniform face they wore and attention-grabbing red lips weren't part of that. Somehow, though, Mona didn't think that the socialite cared too much.

"See you 'round the lot, Good Time Sally," she said, leaving the bathroom and closing Mona in behind her. Alone.

. . .

Two more weeks and no blood. Mona was still having those headaches and dragging through her day wanting to do nothing but lay down and sleep for at least a year or so. She'd also started throwing up regularly, sometimes three or four times in a day. She tried to hide it from the others but she often caught the socialite—whose very apt nickname was Tiny—giving her a strange look when she reappeared, chalk-faced and haggard.

Working with Tiny, Mona had grown almost fond of her. She was a terrible actress and she was definitely a wild thing who didn't give a fig about what anyone else thought, but that was sort of her charm, Mona decided. Tiny was always good for a laugh too, and she had a warmth to her, like a wise older sister who might do your hair and tell you about how to manage boys. Mona'd never really had a sister like that and now, more than ever, she wished that she did.

One day, Mona emerged from the bathroom stall after a particularly miserable episode and found Tiny waiting for her. Stupidly, Mona thought about how her mother would have told Tiny not to frown so much or those creases next to her mouth might stick around.

"You know I was just kidding you before, don't you?" Tiny asked before Mona had a chance to say something. "If you are really hooked on something, I know someone who might be able to help you."

Mona shook her head. "I don't mess around with that."

The two women stood in silence for a moment, Mona staring firmly at her feet. Somehow, she couldn't help but feel as though she were facing down a disappointed teacher. "Have . . . have you ever had any trouble with your monthlies?" Mona asked finally, half-mumbling. She wasn't sure she wanted to tell Tiny but she also didn't know who else she could tell and the problem only seemed to be getting worse.

Tiny gave a relieved chuckle. "Are you kidding? I used to get the worst mood swings when I was a teenager. I once crashed my brother JJ's car through a fence row because he ate the last piece of a peach pie I wanted. Almost gave myself a concussion!" She shook her head fondly. "That was before I discovered reefer."

"No, I meant more like . . . not getting them. Your monthlies, I mean."

"You up the stick?" Tiny peered at her, like she was trying to see through her clothes and her skin.

"No!" Mona said immediately. "I can't be."

Tiny frowned and made those lines appear next to her mouth again. "Honey, you aren't the first gal in a delicate condition to say that."

Mona grabbed her hand impulsively. Startled, Tiny reached out with her other hand and touched Mona's shoulder as though to steady her.

"No," Mona insisted, "I mean I *can't* be pregnant. It's impossible. It's got to be something else."

Tiny nodded though Mona had a feeling that the little woman didn't really agree with her at all. "How late are you?"

"Ten weeks," Mona said, glancing over her shoulder at the closed bathroom door.

"Well, that's not so bad," Tiny said with forced cheer. "Maybe you're just worrying about it too hard. You know what they say about watching pots."

"But nothing like this has ever happened to me before. Ever. You don't think that something might have . . . gone wrong? Down there, I mean?"

The socialite's face softened and she touched the side of Mona's cheek. "No, sweetie, I don't think you're sick. There's lots of reasons a girl might get off track and most of them aren't anything to worry about."

Mona breathed deeply and tried to believe what she was hearing. "I'm sorry," she said. "I'm working a lot of hours right now, I think it's making me cuckoo."

"No worries, cutie. We all have those days, which is why I carry this." The socialite pulled from her purse a slim and elegant flask with her initials (T.M.) engraved upon it. She opened the screw top and offered it to Mona.

What the hell? Mona thought, and took a modest swig. It was certainly one way of getting through the rest of the day.

•   •   •

Another week and nothing, not even a whisper of cramps. Tiny watched her all the time now when she thought that Mona wasn't looking. She didn't ask about her "condition" directly but Mona knew that she was tracking it.

Tiny stopped her one morning before they left wardrobe. She didn't say anything but pulled Mona's costume tightly against her stomach, revealing a small but noticeable bulge in the lowest part of her stomach, right before her private area.

"Mona," Tiny said, so softly. Perhaps it was that very softness but, as she said it, Mona felt something in her crack like an iced-over lake when the spring finally comes.

"Oh sweetie," Tiny said immediately, rummaging in her purse for a handkerchief. "It's gonna be A-okay." She dabbed at Mona's cheeks with her handkerchief and like all of Tiny's things, it was exquisite and fine, the texture smoother and more comforting than any bed Mona had ever slept in or any clothing she had ever worn.

Mona allowed herself to sink down until she was sitting on the bare concrete of the wardrobe area. Tiny crouched down beside her and said in a low voice: "We can get it fixed up." Mona curled herself up tightly and sobbed even harder. It wasn't even sadness she felt, or at least not just sadness. It was terror, confusion and a certain kind of . . . spiritual dread. How had this happened to *her*, of all people?

Tiny tucked her fingers underneath Mona's chin and pushed it upward until Mona could do nothing other than look Tiny in the eye. "Do you understand what I'm saying?"

Mona thought she did, in generalities if not specifically. Mona knew girls who got pregnancies taken care of it. One girl she worked with on the *Little Sally* pictures had three different ones "fixed". "She ought to get *herself* fixed," Mona's mother had said bitterly. "Like any other bitch in heat."

"Tiny," she whispered, "I wasn't lying. It really can't be a baby because I've never been with anyone before."

Tiny's face looked so tragic that, for a moment, Mona thought that she was going to start crying too. "Oh, sweetheart," Tiny said, smoothing her hair, "I know. I know. It counts, though, even if they force you. Even if you don't want it, it can still make a baby."

"I know that!" Mona's voice reverberated off the concrete and the long, gleaming mirror that spanned one side of the room. "I'm not stupid, don't treat me like I'm stupid," Mona hissed.

"Okay, okay, okay," Tiny said. "Now, be quieter or we'll have the cavalry in here after us. I believe you. It's not a baby, then. So we'll take you to a doctor and we'll find out what's what, okay?"

Mona nodded, gulping air painfully into her lungs. "Dry up," Tiny told her, "we're still on call," and Mona couldn't help but laugh at the absurdity of this swinging party girl telling her to get back to work. Impulsively, she reached out and clasped Tiny to her. Tiny returned her hug fiercely, as though she had been made for such things. "We'll get it all sorted," the little woman murmured. "You'll see."

5

Femme Fatale

For a few fleeting seconds, I felt bad that I had ever doubted Connie or her story. She may have had some kooky theories about her grandfather but the tapes were everything she said and more. She had delivered me my personal cave of wonders and I'd accused her of wanting my kidneys.

Pretty quickly, though, all thoughts of Connie (and of the rest of the world) were driven from my mind. As soon as I pressed play, I felt that familiar frisson as the film crackled into life. The movie was in shooting order, not in narrative order, and the sound was low and muted; presumably they planned to remix it later. It was virtually impossible to follow anything like a plot, but I could care less about ninety-nine percent of the characters. I was on the lookout for one singular face and, about fifteen minutes in, I found it.

She wasn't doing much and that was by design—extras were not supposed to draw the viewer's eye after all. She, along with a cluster of other young women, was strolling along in a facsimile of a school hallway. Mona wore a sepulchral uniform and carried a bundle of books. They had styled her hair long and loose and it made her look even younger than her nineteen years. I wondered why she had taken on a role like this—the picture was big but clearly troubled and everything I'd seen about her last days suggested that she was trying for more adult roles to make a cleaner break with her *Little Sally* past.

"Look!" I burst out, excited as a six-year-old girl who had just spotted a horse. "There she is!"

Flavia, who was still sitting next to the open

suitcase puzzling over what appeared to be loose sheets of paper, looked up. "You started it without me?"

"Look," I said again, "there she is, next to the little brunette." Dimly, I registered that something about the little brunette was familiar. Perhaps she was another minor player I had studied? If so, she wasn't a great one—she kept laughing in the middle of takes.

Flavia peered closely at the scene. "She looks sick," she pronounced finally.

"How do you figure?" To my eye, Mona looked much as she had in other films of roughly that period. Her hair was long and vibrant, her face open, her eyes bright.

"Her face just looks . . . worn. Pained, I guess you might say. When was this filmed?"

"Hard to say," I admitted, "but probably pretty early in production. I think this might have been the last film she worked on."

"So this was just a few months before she vanished?" Flavia mused.

On screen, Mona paused and knelt to tie her shoes. The brunette tapped her foot with exaggerated impatience. I was convinced that I knew her from somewhere, though I couldn't imagine why I would have studied her. "Do you recognize her?" I asked, pointing the woman out to Flavia, who shook her head.

Of course it was a longshot asking a dabbler like Flavia to identify a likely extremely obscure extra who probably only did one or two films, but I couldn't exactly avail myself of my considerable resources here so far away from my office. Flavia seemed to have already lost interest, her gaze falling back to her phone.

I kept watching; the next scene was one between Gideon Vale and Lydia Leighton. He kept breaking off midway through, taking on an increasingly frustrated posture every time it happened. The sound quality was too poor to tell exactly what the problem was—a tricky line, perhaps. After one take, Gideon started hitting himself in the head. These weren't exaggerated gestures either—he was hitting his temples and the ridge of his brow with his closed fist and he seemed to be striking pretty hard.

That time, a dumpy little man emerged from off-screen and took his wrists. The dumpy man put his face up close to Vale's and I thought he might be talking softly to him but I couldn't tell.

During each and every one of these odd breaks, Lydia Leighton had the same reaction. Instantly, she shed the skin of character—wide-eyed, young and unconscious of her own appeal—and became shockingly blank. It was so bizarre to watch, like someone had abruptly pulled the batteries from a toy ballerina mid-spin.

"Tiny Malliski," Flavia said suddenly.

"Huh?"

She raised her phone so I could look at the screen, which was a Google Image gallery of the little brunette from the movie. "Huh," I said again, peering at one black and white photo, clearly a scan from a newspaper. The photographer had captured the woman with her head tilted back and her mouth opened in a laugh so visceral that it seemed like I could almost hear it. There was a young man on her arm, smiling dotingly at her and the tiny caption below read "Free wheeling Heiress Tiny Malliski hits the town with "little" brother JJ." "So, was she some kind of starlet?"

"Nope," Flavia said, taking the phone back and scrolling through it again. "She got some kind of murdered."

.   .   .

Apparently the internet had a wealth of information about Tannis "Tiny" Malliski—failed actress, failed singer, failed race car driver and vineyard owner, one-time heiress, and first of the generally agreed upon "Singleton Murders."

Tiny was the much-beloved first child of Jephus Malliski, a former traveling salesman who made his fortune in an unclear fashion. Land speculation was said to be involved. Tiny had two younger brothers, each from a different mother, but Tiny's mother, Sophia, was Jephus's first love. Tiny apparently looked a lot like her mother, who died when she was a small child. Likely it was her physical similarities to her mother that cemented Tiny's place of primacy in her father's heart. By all accounts, he was not a particularly generous man, in the way of men who made their fortunes late in life. But for Tiny, who was already an adolescent when her father became rich, no indulgence was too excessive and no price was too high.

She had access to all of the finest schools (four of which she either left or was kicked out of, depending on the school and who was telling the story) and he provided the start-up funds for her innumerable attempts at a career.

By the time she moved to Los Angeles in 1951, Tiny's primary occupation was "socialite," with a side of "gadabout." She attended parties and dances, wore expensive clothing, and was photographed while doing so. She became moderately famous amongst a certain set but never really rose to the upper echelons of LA society.

In March of '53, just weeks after Mona vanished, Jephus Malinksi Jr (or JJ, as he was commonly called) went to his sister's apartment. He was angry with her; she hadn't answered any of his letters and hadn't taken one of his calls in weeks. Despite her generous allowances from her father, Tiny apparently also owed her brother money, though none of the articles Flavia found said exactly how much money it was or why she owed it.

Nevertheless, JJ apparently wanted to collect so badly that he was willing to fly out from the Malliski family compound in Wyoming to track her down. He likely expected to find her dissipated and distracted, claiming she never got his letters—or perhaps even genuinely oblivious.

"Instead, he discovered her partially dismembered corpse—fuck! That's disgusting," Flavia said. "Whoever this guy was, he was a real fucking sicko.

This says that she was *mostly* in the bathtub. Ugh," Flavia shuddered; I took the phone from her and, to my surprise, she actually let me.

As soon as I finished the paragraph, I understood why. Tiny Malliski, just four foot nine inches tall and not even one-hundred pounds, had been absolutely brutalized. The Wikipedia page listed her injuries in sterile, medical detail but even that detached language gave me an odd, slow chill.

By the time her brother found her, Tiny had been dead for more than a week. Her killer had also made himself at home in her apartment, rifling lazily through her drawers and cupboards. He had even drunk a beer from her fridge, leaving the bottle on the sink and the refrigerator door open. Police theorized that the killer had spent hours, maybe even a whole day, in Tiny's apartment after murdering her.

And they were pretty confident, too, that they knew who that brazen killer was: Tiny's brother JJ. Police theorized that JJ Mallinski had snuck town a week earlier, killed Tiny, and then waited for someone to discover the body. When no one did, he was forced to go himself and make a big production of it. His motive, the police alleged, was this money that he was demanding from Tiny.

This idea quickly fell apart. For one thing, Tiny apparently kept little caches of money everywhere: underneath the top of the toilet tank, taped inside cupboards, under her mattress, in the toes of her shoes, even tucked into the same refrigerator the murderer had availed himself of so casually. All of that money was untouched, despite much of it obviously having been discovered.

Money was clearly not the object of the crime and it seemed unlikely that JJ Malliski, an otherwise utterly unremarkable young man of means, would commit a horrible murder over an unspecified but presumably modest debt. Especially when he could always simply appeal to the real source of wealth in the Malliski family: their father.

As for Jephus himself, he seemed oddly willing to believe that his son might have committed the murder. He allowed JJ to dangle, leaving him without representation in the custody of the LAPD for an astonishing six days. He only ponied up the family's lawyer after details of JJ's detention hit the newspapers. Besides providing a lawyer, Jephus largely stayed out of JJ's case. He did not attend any of his son's court appearances and made no statement when the police officially cleared JJ as a person of interest, despite every other living member of the Malliski clan doing so.

"Weird," Flavia observed, cracking her second energy drink of the evening. "A rich and famous guy *declining* to buy his kid's way out of prison? He knows that's not how that works, right?"

"Well, he's been dead for fifty years now so . . . no, I don't think he knows much of anything."

"It was an obvious joke, dude. But seriously, does it say anything about why he was so hesitant to throw his weight around?"

I scanned the rest of the page. "Not really. Looks like he was pretty tight-lipped about the whole affair.

Maybe he thought JJ did it?" I thought about rich old Jephus, mourning the loss of his first and only daughter, the last piece he had of his most beloved wife. Maybe he needed someone to blame, even though that someone was his own son?

Unfortunately, after clearing JJ Malinksi, the police didn't really have any other ideas to run up the flagpole. They allegedly conducted "hundreds" of interviews with all the types of known criminals you'd expect: the muggers, the rapists, the wife-beaters, and the house-breakers. Nothing led to anything substantial.

And then young Misty Parkington turned up dead. Misty was a cocktail waitress at a popular nightspot in the city, *The Paper Lantern*. Like Tiny Mallinski, she was brown-haired and pretty but that was about where the comparisons stopped. Misty was firmly working-class with two young children to support. Her husband was out of the picture and she worked constantly, sometimes up to three jobs at a time to keep a roof over their heads.

It was hard to imagine the circumstances under which Tiny Mallinski and Misty Parkington would have shared a cab, let alone a killer. And yet, there was a strong belief from the beginning of the investigation that the two cases were linked. Misty was also murdered in her home and the killer had similarly made himself free with her space, eating her food and flipping through the books on the bookshelf. He'd left her oven door open, as though he'd paused to reheat something.

Like Tiny, Misty was also, as the papers said then "outraged." She had been killed in an unnecessarily gruesome fashion, her body left out in clear view, as Tiny's had been.

What made Misty's case all the more remarkable, however, was the fact that her son and daughter were asleep in their bedroom while the whole thing happened. They were no more than ten feet away from the murder, though the papers said that neither child recalled hearing or seeing anything out of the ordinary. They hadn't even woken up, apparently. Police theorized that this might have been because there was nothing to hear—both Tiny and Misty lacked anything in the way of defensive wounds and though someone had clearly been in both of their homes, there was no sign that a physical struggle had taken place.

Misty was followed by Soledad Gonzales and Angela Carey, both butchered in their homes by someone who seemed to have no concern whatsoever about being caught in the midst of a crime. The papers started calling the crimes "The Singleton Murders" because each of the women was unmarried, though only Tiny actually lived alone.

"The city's young women are encouraged to buddy up and be *smart*," Flavia read. "Real helpful, fuckers. I'm sure the buddy system would have saved all these women from getting dismembered in their own homes. Also, way to suggest that the girls died because they were *dumb*, I'm sure that was comforting for the families."

"It was 1953," I pointed out.

"Yeah, and the playbook hasn't changed all that much," Flavia scowled.

From the defensive tone of the police statements, public concern with the Singleton Murders was sky high. Then, like a cloud that blows briefly across the sun before vanishing into the horizon, it all stopped.

No more murders, no more tortured bodies, no more bizarre home invasions.

And no solutions.

It was one of the great unsolved LA mysteries, though the only reason I'd ever heard of it—heard of Tiny—was because it all started not two months after Mona vanished. Sometimes bloggers would theorize that Mona was another Singleton victim but, most commonly, they simply mentioned her case as part of the "atmosphere" in the city leading up to the murders.

Mona didn't really fit in with the other Singleton victims. She was seemingly taken from a public place, not attacked in her own home. Her body appeared to have been deliberately concealed, whereas whoever had slain Tiny and the others seemed content to leave their messes out in the open. Neither did Mona appear to be this killer's physical "type." All of the others were petite brunettes while Mona was a statuesque blonde. Or redhead, depending on how one defines "redhead."

People went back and forth on the case (or cases) all the time. Some said it was a nascent serial killer and connected it to all sorts of other deaths in the city at that time. Others claimed it was merely a series of sad but not atypical "domestics" that got blown out of proportion by a city in panic. Still others seemed to think it was a bit of both, a real predator with some unrelated crimes thrown in.

"But they knew each other," Flavia said. "They worked on the same movie and then a few months later Mona goes missing and Tiny is dead. That's not a coincidence, right?"

"That's also not related to what we're doing here," I reminded her. "We're studying their films, not solving their murders."

Flavia didn't say anything but, unsurprisingly, she was very bad at not saying anything. "What?" I asked her finally because it was very clear that we weren't going to talk about anything else until she said her piece.

"Okay, so, Connie's grandpa, right? He must have been around for this production. At the very least, we know he saw the footage. So that means that he's linked to not one but two women who died under mysterious circumstances. That's kinda fucked up, right?"

"Are you saying that Connie's grandpa was a serial killer?" If the next sentence out of her mouth contained the words "Zodiac Killer," I was going to kick her ass out of the room and I didn't care what she did about it.

"He has footage of both women."

"He has an unfinished film they both acted in! You're talking like he planted a hidden camera in their toilet or something."

"*I'm* not the one who brought the whole murderous grandpa into this," she said pointedly.

"No, you're not and you're also not an investigator so get off that grandpa's case, Columbo."

"Columbo! God, you are the oldest twenty-one year old in the world."

• • •

I left off *The Redfield House* then. There were clearly many more hours of footage and I wanted to take a more holistic look at the tapes before I settled in to sift through it all. Whether or not Connie's grandfather had been a depraved killer, he did have a connoisseur's eye when it came to Mona's work. He had copies of some of her earliest shorts, ones she hadn't even been credited in when she appeared only as part of a school classroom or in a long-shot crowd scene. He had two of the lost *Little Sally* movies, including *Little Sally and the Ghost* where Mona's character played an abnormally large part, learning to overcome her fear of the dark in an improbable climactic scene set at a lighthouse.

There was also another footage shot, I suspected, during the filming of *Shores of Desire*. According to Connie's timeline, that would have been when her grandfather first met Mona and he had apparently shot some amateur behind the scenes stuff with what was probably an eight millimeter camera.

When the film went into production in 1951, Mona was still a teenager and she looked it. She showed off her styled hair and her costume for the camera, smoked countless cigarettes, performed short, nonsensical dances between takes, and laughed frequently.

There were more unsettling moments, though, when Mona did not appear to be aware that the camera was watching her as she pored over a script or dabbed at her makeup in a mirror. There was one particularly creepy segment filmed through what appeared to be the partially opened door of the dressing room.

"Yeah," Flavia said, "nothing weird or skeevy about these tapes at all."

"You really think that he could have done that? That anyone could have done that? Slaughter half a dozen women and then just . . . retire to Reseda and raise a family?"

Flavia shook her head, watching the Mona on-screen who tilted her head first to one side and then the other, a parody of the impish little girl she'd played in the *Little Sally* movies. "I believe that people are capable of anything," she said. "The weirdest thing you can imagine, the worst thing you can imagine, someone has done it."

We both watched the TV then. The scene had changed. It was Mona on the lot, smoking a cigarette and looking up. The footage was all in black and white but I could tell it was a sunny day. It was so bright that she squinted; so bright that she had to raise her hand to protect herself.

6

Waste of a Rabbit

Tiny wasn't kidding about her doctor being tight-lipped. He barely said two words to them the whole time they were at the clinic and didn't even greet them when he came into the exam room. Mona had thought up a fake name to give him (Susan Johnson) but he never even asked. Instead he just nodded grimly at her and gestured toward a paper dress folded on the exam table.

At least he let Tiny stay in the room. Mona thought that people probably let Tiny do pretty much whatever she wanted a lot of the time. Tiny folded her clothes for her while Mona inched her way up the table. It was the first time in Mona's life she hadn't had to wait for a doctor. She and Tiny hadn't even seen the waiting room, in fact. A woman that Mona presumed to be the doctor's nurse had ushered them directly from the street through a back hallway and into the examination room.

It was still just as uncomfortable as any other doctor's office, however: the air always just a few degrees off pleasant, the metal of instruments or surfaces just a bit too bright and steely.

"I told him everything you told me," Tiny informed her, reaching over to pat her hand. "About your mom and about how you haven't had any . . . activity yet."

Still, the doctor's disinterest was palpable when he came back into the room after the most cursory of knocks. He didn't spare a glance for Mona's face, heading instead straight to her legs which he manipulated in an utterly dispassionate fashion, placing her feet into the stirrups. He was neither particularly gentle nor unduly rough—he handled her the way a farmer might manipulate a dairy cow. Mona fought the urge to clamp her legs closed. To focus, she stared at the top of the doctor's head where the faintest glimmers of pink scalp was starting to show through his dark hair.

Tiny stood beside her, clasping her hand as the doctor examined her, a series of cold pressures and the occasional bright stab of pain. Once he made a little huffing sound, as though someone was lingering in front of him in a line, and Mona felt a burst of warm hurt that made her eyes water.

He withdrew just as abruptly, looking sternly at Mona through her own crooked knees. He stood up and walked around side her, pulling up the side of her gown and feeling her stomach all over with quick, pointed fingers. He frowned and reached down for his stethoscope, putting the bulbs in his ears and the cold metal eye flat on her belly.

"You're pregnant," he said finally. "I can send away for a test if you insist but it would be a waste of time and a rabbit. I'd say you're about three months gone."

"Do the test," Tiny said immediately. Mona could not help but imagine her as one of those minuscule little dogs who have no real sense of their own size relative to that of their opponent.

The doctor withdrew a small paper tablet from his pocket. "You'll be paying then, I suppose?" His voice was carefully neutral but Mona knew from living an entire life with Momma and Rita how someone could cut and insinuate without ever speaking in any but the blandest tones.

Sure enough, Tiny looked a little bit quelled. She had no immediate response for the doctor, which told them all that she was not, in fact, planning on paying for the test.

Mona reached up and rested a hand on her forearm.

"No," she said softly. "There's no need."

The doctor put his notebook back in his pocket with a decisive air, as though with that single gesture, he had wrapped up all of Mona's difficulties and tucked them away. "Good afternoon, girls," he said, already on his way out the door.

* * *

Tiny's apartment was in a good-but-not-amazing part of town and it was only two bedrooms. The only real nod toward decadence, in fact, was that second bedroom, which she apparently used as an enormous closet for her considerable wardrobe.

"You want something to eat?" Tiny asked, opening and closing the kitchen cupboards in a small gesture of uselessness. Mona sat down on Tiny's sedate little loveseat and shook her head.

"I'll have some water," Mona said, "if you've got it."

Tiny gave her a wry look. "I think it can be found." Nevertheless, she busied herself at the sink for longer than necessary to give Mona time to pause and collect herself.

"Here you go, kiddo" she said finally, sitting beside Mona and handing her a glass tumbler.

Mona sipped the water and looked out Tiny's window to avoid looking at her face. Mona had a feeling that if she looked at Tiny and saw the pity in her eyes, she would start crying. "I've been over here before. Worked at *The Paper Lantern*."

"I've never been," Tiny admitted. Mona looked at her, startled.

"I woulda thought you'd been everywhere that mattered in this city."

Tiny smiled but it was altogether unlike her usual big grin. This was just a little creep upwards of the corners of her mouth. "I don't get out much," she said, "if you can believe it."

Mona snorted. "I don't know if I can. Most of the time you come in still smelling like gin."

"Not going out don't mean I can't have a drink," Tiny laughed. "I'm not much for it, the parties and the nightlife. Not anymore. I feel like . . . I did all that already, you know?" Tiny laughed again, sounding rueful this time. "You won't believe it, but I actually came to LA to get away from that sort of thing."

"How long you been here?"

"Couple of years," Tiny shrugged. "I came out when I was twenty-five." Mona nodded absently. She hadn't realized Tiny was that old, pushing thirty, even.

"Look, I know that Dr. Winston is a bit of an ass and I'm sorry he was so short with you but he is the only one in the city I'd trust if you want to get it taken care of."

Mona turned to her, giving her a goggle-eyed stare.

"Not that you have to," Tiny added quickly. "You can do as you like. I just thought . . . if you wanted to do something about it, you might want to do it before the baby gets bigger."

Bigger. That was a terrifying word. The idea of her body popping outward, thickening and swelling no matter what she ate or what she purged; Mona wasn't sure she could cope with that. But she wasn't sure she could cope with the alternative either.

"I don't know if I could do that." Mona tried to imagine what her mother might have told her. On one hand, Momma would have thought her a bad and stupid girl for getting into this mess in the first place. On the other hand, Mona's mother always said that it was her own pregnancy that had ruined her body and shut her out forever from the pictures. In the end, Mona thought Momma would tell her the same thing she had always told her, both in word and action: do what you need to do for your career.

"Is it . . . I mean, I've heard things," Mona said hesitantly. "You know, we all hear things. About it being real dangerous."

Tiny shook her head. "It is, if you're doing it yourself or going to some creep. Girls die from that sort of shit. But if you've got a real doctor, it's different. If you go in early, he can take it all out in an afternoon. It feels like you're having a real bad period." Tiny put an arm around her. "I'll even go with you, if you like."

"You've done it?" Mona asked and Tiny nodded at

her. She didn't seem the worse for wear but Tiny was the sort of woman who could manage these things. Sophisticated, mature, and rich, Tiny seemed like someone who could cope with just about anything.

"That's how I met Dr. Winston. I didn't want to do it somewhere folks knew me and all my people."

"It . . . happened back home?" Mona realized suddenly that she had no idea where Tiny was from originally. This woman who now knew so much about her—things no one else knew, in fact—and they were still mostly strangers to one another.

"Mercury, Wyoming. I got myself in trouble with . . . a man I loved very much. Though I shouldn't have."

"He run out on you?" Mona was very familiar with that story. She had wondered over the years if their mother's strident insistence that she had been married to their father before the twins' conception wasn't a cover for a sadder story.

Tiny shook her head. "No. It was more complicated than that. It wasn't something . . . you know how some plants are so delicate that if you move them from one sort of room to another, they'll wither up? Like the smallest change in the temperature or the light is gonna kill them dead? That's what it was between me and him."

"Did he know about the baby?"

Tiny hesitated. "He did eventually." The way she said it told Mona clearly that she wasn't interested in discussing her mystery fella's reaction. That, at least, was one thing that Mona didn't have to worry about. Maybe it would have been better if she did, though. A man could be convinced to pitch in some dough, maybe, even if he wasn't wild about it.

Instead, Mona was alone. Even Tiny, who seemed to understand so much, could only stretch herself so far, not all the way into Mona's shoes.

"You don't believe that I never went with a man, do you?" Mona asked.

"I . . . don't know what to believe," Tiny admitted. "I don't think you're lying to me," she added quickly, seeing the look on Mona's face. "But we both know that what you're talking about just isn't possible. Unless you're the Virgin Mary or something. You'd tell me, though, if any angels came to you recently, wouldn't you?"

Tiny smiled and, with considerable effort, Mona managed to smile back.

. . .

Three buses and a ten-minute walk later, Mona was back home.

In all that time, though, she couldn't seem to shake Tiny's words. No, an angel hadn't come to visit her. At least, she didn't think they had. But would she know if she had been . . . visited? Infected? By something otherworldly?

Mona searched her memory for anything strange or out of the ordinary in her life but there was nothing she could recall. Her days were the same reel of work and home and more work, anxiety and striving and hunger.

The only thing she could remotely think of was a thing that was neither new nor unusual, something that had dogged her for a while now, since around the time Momma got sick: the bad dreams. The *heavy* dreams, weighted with a kind of . . . presence, like someone hovering over her. Occasionally that unnamed presence would press down on her, cover her mouth with heat and weight. She would wake up gasping and that first inhalation always ached.

She had thought that it was stress about her lack of work, fear over her mother's condition and what would become of them all, but could it be something else? Was that what . . . annunciation felt like? Suffocation? Looming death?

She could not deny that when she thought now about the unstoppable growing thing in her belly, her primary feeling was that same sense of something heavy bearing down on her and choking the life from her.

They had a bible somewhere in the house. Mona was sure of it, though she could not say exactly where.

They had never been what one might call a god-fearing family. Mona tore apart the lone bookcase in the house. She checked every drawer and end table, even creeping into Rita and Clark's room to examine their dresser.

She finally found it in possibly the oddest of locations, half-tucked under the edge of her mother's sofa bed. She could not imagine how it had wound up there. It was not the sort of thing that Rita would think to provide and her mother had not gotten up and walked around without assistance in weeks. And yet, there it was, "Holy Bible" embossed upon the cover in flaking gold, the pages thinner even than newsprint.

Inside the cover, there was a pointed scrawl, a list of names and birth dates that stopped with her mother's name and birthdate in 1908. The very first (James L. McKee) had a birthdate of 1789.

The bible was unwieldy for an unfamiliar reader. Mona struggled through many incomprehensible passages before finally stumbling upon what she believed to be the plight of Mary, a girl who found herself with child despite never knowing a man.

And the angel came in unto her, and said, Hail, thou that art highly favoured, the Lord is with thee: blessed art thou among women.

Mary had been offered the gift of clarity, at least. No one had spoken so directly to Mona—or spoken at all. Shouldn't a blessing also come with an explanation?

And when she saw him, she was troubled at his saying, and cast in her mind what manner of salutation this should be.

This seemed a very mild reaction to Mona, but perhaps in bible days people were more at home with God working directly in their lives. Perhaps angel messengers were a dime a dozen, like a singing telegram?

And the angel said unto her, Fear not, Mary: for thou hast found favour with God. And, behold,

thou shalt conceive in thy womb, and bring forth a
son, and shalt call his name Jesus.

One would think that Mary at least would have
gotten to name her child. But the angel was very
clear: despite growing in her body, the baby would
not belong to her in any meaningful way. Mona felt
an odd sort of relief at that idea. It would be nice to
think that the thing inside her was for something else,
for *someone* else.

Then said Mary unto the angel, How shall this
be, seeing I know not a man?

And the angel answered and said unto her, The
Holy Ghost shall come upon thee, and the power
of the Highest shall overshadow thee: therefore also
that holy thing which shall be born of thee shall be
called the Son of God.

Reading this, Mona had a moment of the most
absurd sort of jealousy. A teenage girl, dead now
for more than a thousand years, and she envied her.

Because Mary was allowed to ask questions and receive at least some manner of answer.

Then there was something about Mary's elderly infertile cousin also getting up the spout, but at least that woman had presumably fooled around with her husband. The angel reassured her that this was all God's work that, with Him "nothing shall be impossible" and Mary seemed to find that comforting, or at least definitive because the next part read:

And Mary said, Behold the handmaid of the Lord; be it unto me according to thy word. And the angel departed from her.

Mona let the book fall flat on her thighs. This was stupid, all of this. She was not a handmaid of the Lord. She was not beloved by God. This was not part of anyone's plan, divine or otherwise.

7

Madonna/Whore

"**W**hat was in the suitcase?" I asked when dim yellow light started to creep through the partially-closed curtains. We'd been up all night but we'd worked through a lot of the footage, save for the incredible undertaking that was *The Redfield House.*

"Clothes," Flavia said, rubbing her eyes. She'd had four of those energy drinks and I told her she should pace herself but she just laughed and pointed at my ravaged mini-bar. "A couple of outfits, nothing you could run away and start a new life with.

A shitload of sanitary napkins, though. Geez, those things are gnarly."

I chuckled. "I thought your whole brand was built on nostalgia for the past?"

"Artistic appreciation is not the same as nostalgia. Trust me, I know exactly how shitty 1953 would have been for a brown girl." She pointed at the television screen, which was paused on a frame from one of Mona's first *Little Sally* movies. She couldn't have been more than six or seven. "Look what 1953 did to her."

"And what about the weird writings Connie mentioned?"

Flavia leaned over the edge of the bed and grabbed something from the still-opened suitcase. "See for yourself," she said, handing me a few sheets of loose paper.

The first one was addressed to "Rita and Momma." It read:

Remember that I love you and that everything

I've done has been for the best, even if it doesn't feel that way. I hope you can forgive me for all of this.

Your Mona.

"Who is Rita anyway?" Flavia asked.

"Mona's twin."

"Mona had a *twin*? Was she in pictures too?"

"Fraternal twin," I said. I had seen photographs of Rita McKee and while she was hardly ugly, she wasn't exactly the movie star type either. She was tall like Mona and they had the same thick, red-blonde hair but that was about where the similarities ended. Rita had a sturdy, athletic build and significant scarring on her face and neck from a childhood case of chicken pox.

She also had a pretty severe case of what would be today called "resting bitch face." By all accounts, Rita wanted nothing to do with the Hollywood scene and less than a year after Mona vanished, she lost her husband in some sort of gun cleaning accident. After that, she had moved out of LA and lived an unremarkable life in the central coast region.

"I thought she might be another actress," Flavia mused, "because of the second letter." She pointed at the papers in my hands and I shuffled them until I had the relevant pages. The second letter was less straightforward and altogether weirder than the first, starting with the address:

For Tiny

Thank you so much for everything. None of this is your fault. I would have gone to Dr. Winston if I could have but I wouldn't ever have taken your money. You've already been kinder than I deserve.

-Mona

"What the fuck?" I muttered. "Why would she be taking money from Tiny?"

Together, the two notes did have a bit of a

"goodbye cruel world" vibe to them. Had Mona gotten sick? Did this Dr. Winston tell her that she had some incurable disease? Did she want to spare her family the burden of another invalid?

"Probably for an abortion," Flavia said breezily.

"Oh come on." That was one of the many knee-jerk reactions to Mona's case—to any case, really, when a woman disappeared before the passage of Roe v. Wade—it must have been a botched abortion and an illegal body dump. That ignored the particulars of Mona's life, however. Not only did she not have any romantic attachments at the time of her death, she'd never had such a relationship, something that she made very clear in her diaries. "She was only nineteen."

"Nineteen year olds have sex. I mean, it sounds like you probably didn't, but it has been known to happen," Flavia said.

When I was nineteen, I was in the midst of completing my master's degree. My closest colleagues were five to seven years older than me, and many of them were in long-term relationships. Some even had children. It was hardly the raucous free-for-all that was the "average" college experience (at least from what I could tell).

I imagined it had to have been similar for Mona. In her diaries, she wrote about nearly always being the youngest person in the room, about requiring extra rules, guardians, and protocols to be a child in an adult world. Her mother was almost pathological in her vigilance about her daughter's safety and Mona herself was shockingly shy and anxious and, in the months before her death, everyone agreed that she was working constantly. When did she have the time to even date, let alone become pregnant out of wedlock?

"There's no mention of any kind of boyfriend in her diaries."

When I said "diaries," Flavia perked up oddly. She gave me a surprised look but quickly turned her face down, tapping something into her phone.

"I dunno man, it does seem like there's some

support for that theory," Flavia shook her head and began reading aloud from something she'd found on her phone. "Prominent local doctor fingered in abortion ring scandal. Dr. Harlow Winston of Beverly Hills was identified today as part of the Reed-Fuller crime ring which performed terminations on as many as four hundred women in our city." She started scrolling faster through the article with her thumb. "Degenerate criminals, dangerous practices, blah, blah, blah . . . Looks like he denied being affiliated with the other people. One was, like, a med student and the other was just a woman. No credentials or anything. Winston was an actual doctor at least."

She stopped abruptly, her eyes widened. "Oh shit."

"What? Let me see," I peered over her shoulder. The print was tiny but I could see the picture at the top of the article. Two pictures in fact, one a grim mugshot of an older white man with small spectacles and the other that familiar laughing portrait of Tiny Malliski (this time with her brother cropped out).

"He says he performed an abortion on Tiny and other high-profile women," Flavia breathed. "Dude, I'm totally right about this. Mona was pregs, Tiny tried to send her to her doctor but it didn't work out."

I shook my head. "But how did that happen?"

"Probably the usual way, I'd imagine."

"I mean, who was the father? Mona worked constantly and spent her nights at home with her family. Where would she meet a man?"

Flavia stared down at the phone but, for the first time, I got the impression that she wasn't so much looking at it as avoiding looking at me. "Maybe it wasn't a love affair. Maybe it was an assault. That can happen pretty fast and it can happen anywhere. Work, home, wherever."

On the television screen, Mona still a pudgy-limbed child reached out for her costar, her arms open and empty. Had her misfortunes begun even before that day in February when she vanished off the face of the earth?

"I hope that didn't happen," I said finally, softly.

"I hope so too," Flavia agreed. She still wouldn't look up from her phone.

• • •

As much as I knew that it was not my job to ferret out what had happened to Mona, as much as I reminded myself that I was supposed to be paying attention to the films, I couldn't shake the questions. Mona was not a wholly academic subject to me; she never had been. The idea of someone assaulting her and leaving her pregnant out of wedlock in the early 1950s was too horrible—too unfair—to contemplate.

I wanted to ask Connie a bit more about her grandfather, his personality, and the family lore about him, but when I called down to the front desk to get her room number I was surprised to learn that she had already checked out.

"Man, she's burning rubber," Flavia snorted.

Thankfully, she'd also put a business card in the bag with the tapes and it listed her cell phone. I had to call three times before she actually answered and I could hear the sound of people talking in the background.

"Did you . . . just leave?" I asked.

Connie sighed. "I left, yes. Because there was no reason to stay." She didn't ask who was calling; it seemed like she'd been expecting me.

"Well, I wanted to ask you some questions."

"Yeah? Talk fast, my flight boards in forty minutes."

She even had a flight lined up? Somehow, the idea made me uneasy. She'd bought a pass to the conference and airfare to and from the city all to give me a bunch of videos and then vanish? It made me feel like, somehow, we'd made some kind of deal and I'd gotten the short end.

"Is there any chance that your grandfather could have gotten Mona pregnant?"

Connie was silent for a long time but I knew the call hadn't been dropped because I could still hear airport noise in the background. "Whatever happened between him and Mona, it . . . hurt my grandmother. I don't think she ever really recovered. They stayed married but Mom always said they weren't happy and it wasn't a secret. They only ever got married in the first place because he knocked up Grandma when she was a teenager. I wouldn't think he'd make the same mistake twice and, well, I've always thought that Mona was pretty out of Grandpa Gene's league."

"Grandpa Gene?" I didn't remember Connie ever telling me her grandfather's name before. "What was his last name?"

"Some long Russian name, at least originally. He wrote under Gene Vincent, though."

"Gene Vincent," I said dully. Across the room, Flavia mouthed *"What the fuck?"* at me.

"Yeah like the, you know, like in the note."

"You think Mona meant your grandfather when she wrote *GV knows?*"

Again, Connie was silent for a long time. "I think my granddad's name was Gene Vincent. I think he was someone who was . . . aggrieved about his life and I think something happened the year Mona disappeared that ruined my grandparents' marriage. Made it hateful and bitter. Made it so Grandma cried when she watched those old movies."

This had ruined Connie's family I realized. Not in grand dramatic fashion that they made movies about but in the small, shabby, ordinary way that secrets fester and resentments accrue. The fallout had filtered down to affect even Gene Vincent's granddaughter. Whatever happened to Mona, whatever Vincent did or didn't do, it wouldn't change the scars he'd left on his family.

"Why are you asking me about Mona being pregnant? Are you thinking she had a baby?"

"No," I said. "I don't think she did."

．　．　．

"So Grandpa Vincent was GV, huh?" Flavia mused as soon as I hung up the phone.

"He was *a* GV, not necessarily *the* GV. And there's no evidence that the notation in her purse was at all related to her disappearance."

Flavia held her hands up in mock-surrender. "Chill, dude. I'm not saying it's definitive, just that it's . . . notable. I always thought that GV was Vale anyway. The police barely glanced at him and he was off the rails in the early fifties."

She wasn't entirely wrong. I'd never specifically studied Gideon Vale but I knew his story generally. Most scholars believed he was struggling with some sort of mental illness combined with likely some substance abuse and his behavior became more and more erratic in the years before he died.

Working through the unused *Redfield House* footage had brought that idea to vivid life—it also explained exactly why the film wound up sitting on the shelf. Gideon Vale was very clearly floundering and he was also clearly the reason that the film was going over time and budget.

Gideon Vale was fascinating even when he was falling apart, however. He had that star quality, that ability to draw the eye even when he was having a bizarre, almost inhuman meltdown. In fact, that very mercurial quality made him more compelling. He could turn nearly instantly from the leading man I remembered from countless films—effortlessly debonair, inescapably masculine, supremely confident—to a crumpled, anxious husk.

I was fascinated, as well, by Lydia Leighton's reaction. Or, rather, her complete lack of a reaction. Gideon Vale and Lydia Leighton were one of the great sweeping romances of Hollywood's golden age. They were together from Lydia's early career in the late '30s to Gideon's 1958 death in a house fire. There were all sorts of stories and rumors about them—they had odd sexual predilections and both carried on multiple affairs. It was a studio-mandated relationship that morphed into something deeper and more codependent. One or more of them was unable to have children and it poisoned their relationship. There were even those who suspected that Lydia had something to do with the fire that killed Gideon. It was ruled an accident but stories of arson and murder persisted.

I had always believed, though, that Lydia Leighton was the last person who would want Gideon dead. It was true that he was notoriously erratic in his final years but that was more of a problem for the studio than for Lydia. Lydia needed Gideon; her pictures without him were all notorious flops.

There was such an emptiness to Lydia in this footage, though. No sense at all that she was concerned for her partner of more than fifteen years. The only time she evinced any emotion was when, in the midst of an episode, Gideon drew too closely to her. When that happened, she cringed back, pulling her arms tightly against her body and tilting her head down, like a boxer preparing to take a hit.

Usually, these outbursts happened during one of Gideon's scenes. I noticed, however, that as the film marched onward, his interference was obvious even in moments when his character was not on-screen. There would be scenes that abruptly stopped, actors looking between each other in confusion and then back out at something beyond the scope of the camera. I was confident that whatever they were looking at was Vale-related.

"What do you think it meant, then, if it was about Vale? What was he supposed to have known?" I asked.

Flavia shrugged and gave a deep yawn. "Baby, I guess? I read a couple of bios that suggested he'd gotten physical with Lydia Leighton, doesn't sound like the kind of dude who would take a pregnant mistress in stride."

"I don't know . . . " From what I'd seen in the videos, Gideon wasn't cogent enough to have something on the side, let alone get rid of her so completely that she remained a missing person sixty years later.

"Okay, I'm crashing," Flavia said, curling into a fetal position on the opposite side of the bed. "But I'm gonna wake up in an hour. Don't watch anything important without me."

"Sure, *boss*."

"I mean it." Flavia stabbed her index finger at me. "When this conference is over, you're gonna have all the time in the world with those tapes. All I have is right now, these three days. If something interesting happens, you've gotta wake me up."

• • •

Something interesting happened. I did not wake her up.

In my defense, it all happened very quickly and during what appeared to be another endless series of reshoots on a simple scene in *The Redfield House*. Then, abruptly, Gideon Vale entered the frame.

The extras—including Mona—seemed as surprised as I was. Most of them froze and looked to Lydia, who had gone blank again and was waiting, as she always did, for it to be over. Gideon was angry, the kind of uncontrolled anger of a child that seems inextricably connected to every other bodily function—weeping, nausea, pain. There was a muffled sound, like someone yelling through a wad of fabric, and I thought it was coming from Vale.

Two of the extras sidled out of frame, leaving Mona, one other girl, and Lydia. Mona was watching Gideon warily and he too seemed to have taken notice of her. He said something to her and Mona looked off-screen, seeking the approval of some invisible person. She said something then that I could not make out but it had a strong effect on Gideon.

He sank to his knees in front of her. Mona's face was alarmed but she didn't move or retreat the way Lydia did when Gideon got too close.

Gideon reached out and grabbed Mona by the hips, pulling her forward into him violently, and Mona stumbled, almost fell, but Gideon leaned his face and chest into her torso and halted her fall. Mona was frozen, with shock and something like embarrassment on her face. Of course she was embarrassed—what Gideon was doing was practically an obscenity in 1953.

He had pressed his face into the area just above her mons pubis and wrapped his arms around her lower hips so she could not free herself. He ground his forehead against her, looking for all the world as though he were performing an odd, fully-clothed sex act upon an alarmed Mona. She held her hands up, arms in the air as though she did not know what to do with them. She kept looking off camera beseechingly.

Finally, the dumpy little man came and put a steadying hand on Gideon's shoulder. He pulled Vale away from Mona, though Gideon remained on his knees. His face was tilted up at Mona's face and it appeared he was saying something to her but the back of his head was to the camera and I couldn't make out his expression.

Mona's expression, however, was very clear and rapidly shifting. From that shock and fear and confusion, her face softened like warm candle wax. She looked down at Vale with huge eyes and her face, it was . . . grateful?

He reached a hand up as though to touch her again but I did not see how she reacted because the scene cut then to a banal scene of Lydia's character talking to a female teacher.

I looked at Flavia, who had drooled a dark cloud into the pillow around her mouth. An assault could happen in a moment, she had said. It could happen at work. It could happen with all of Mona's co-workers around and who would have stopped it? Who would have stopped the biggest male star of the age from doing whatever he wanted to do?

Who *could* have stopped him?

8

Visitations

"You know that I would do anything for you," Gene told her, but Mona had not known that, in fact. She had always considered Gene a casual friend, at most—they'd only ever actually worked together twice. "If you need money, I can get it for you."

She *did* need money. Tiny's doctor and his clean office, his discreet street entrance, did not come cheap. Tiny herself couldn't help. She had confessed to Mona that her father had more or less cut her off when she moved to Los Angeles.

"Daddy'll come around eventually," she had

assured Mona. "This isn't the first time I've done something to make him mad. But it was a pretty bad thing, may take longer than usual for him to remember that he loves me."

In the meantime, Tiny was just another girl in the city, trying to keep her lights on.

In theory, there were other folks in the city, doctors and otherwise, who could help her, but Mona wasn't entirely comfortable with the idea. Going to a med student or a veterinarian or just someone's old grandmother scared her deep down in her bones. If she bled out in someone's backroom or bathroom, who would take care of Momma and Rita and the mortgage?

There was also the fact that she didn't even know how to find these . . . other avenues, even if she wanted to. She had been lucky in that Tiny was both the only person she had told about her predicament and also the only person she knew who had access to the kind of doctor she needed. She hadn't even really told Gene was what happening, only that she was having family troubles and might be away for a couple of days.

Mona didn't exactly relish the idea of disclosing her condition to other people and, even if she did, who could she possibly ask for help? Rita? Her bedridden mother? The other extras she knew only in passing? Tiny had stuck her neck out, taking Mona to the doctor's office. Could she really ask someone else, almost certainly a stranger, to do the same thing? She had a feeling if Gene knew exactly why she needed money, he might well rescind his offer. This was not the sort of thing that men took kindly to, in Mona's limited experience, unless they themselves were implicated in the outcome.

And, on top of all this, she didn't have much time to ruminate on all of this. If she was indeed about three months along, as Dr. Winston suggested (and as her own record-keeping confirmed) it would not be long before she started showing in a more definitive way. She had to act quickly if she wanted to keep all of this a secret.

Gene's offer of money seemed to be the best answer to her problem, but was it really? Writers were better paid than extras but not by much and Gene was hardly setting Hollywood afire with his scripts. Also, Mona knew that he had a wife and a small child to support.

"I can't . . . I can't take your money, Gene," she managed finally and Gene looked somewhat disappointed. "I'll manage." *Somehow*, Mona thought.

"Well, be sure to let me know if you need anything. A place to stay, shoulder to cry on." He reached out and took her hands warmly, like a sister. Mona almost cried as he squeezed her fingers together. What had she done to deserve these kind folks who treated her better than her own family did?

"Thank you," she said, her voice catching in her throat. "You can't know what that means to me."

• • •

"An . . . installment plan?" Dr. Winston looked at her as though she'd slapped a bloody dead chicken down on his desk.

"Yes," Mona said, convulsively straightening the bottom of her jacket. She had worn her audition outfit, her dourest, most professional clothing.

"Miss Johnson, a termination is not like buying a refrigerator or a sedan. If you, for example, stop paying me, I cannot simply put the fetal material back in your womb."

His tone was sharp as a slap. "Dr. Winston, I assure you, I'm very responsible. I've never been in debt in my life. I've been supporting my family since I was eight years old." The more she spoke, the less he seemed to hear her. He sat across from her behind his desk, his face bland and unaffected.

"I saw you as a favor to Miss Malliski," he said. "Under ordinary circumstances, I would not have allowed you in my clinic. I have to maintain a certain type of clientele, Miss Johnson, because what I do is dangerous and someone like you is a bad risk, I'm afraid."

A bad risk because she did not have an important family like Tiny? Or enough money to make it worthwhile? Or because she was the kind of lunatic who claimed to have gotten pregnant as a virgin?

Mona supposed her face must have looked particularly stricken because Dr. Winston seemed uncomfortable. It was the first time she had seen him look anything less than cool and competent. "There are other practitioners," he told her. "Some are even quite reputable. And you will find them far more willing to accept alternate forms of payment."

And what "alternate" sources of payment are these to be? she wondered. But his face told her all she needed to know. There were men in the city who would get rid of the thing inside her in exchange for the "form of payment" that all young women possessed. After all, the baby in her belly proved she was the sort of girl who did that kind of thing.

She should have thought of something, some

withering condemnation to leave him with, but there was nothing in her head except a great rushing noise. It was exactly the sort of thing that would happen to her when she was girl and Rita tormented her in some way. No comeback leapt to her lips, no motion to her limbs. She was frozen by her own pain and by that little foolish feeling of surprise that someone would hurt her like that, though she knew, of course, that the world was full of hurting.

And, if she was being very honest with herself, she did not think she could entirely afford to alienate Dr. Winston. Even now, with everything he had told her, if he offered to do the termination for her, she would accept his offer. The space between the rock and the hard place was miserable indeed.

●　●　●

When Mona got home from her appointment, her sister was already there. This was highly unusual—generally Rita did not finish work before seven.

Mona also had the sense that Rita did not like to be alone with their mother. If she had a free afternoon, she was far more likely to spend it window-shopping or strolling around a park than rushing home to sit in silence with the dying woman.

Rita seemed surprised to see her as well. "Audition?" She asked, taking in Mona's outfit and her undoubtedly dejected expression.

"It didn't go well," Mona said. "I won't be called back."

Rita, seated at the table with a steaming cup in front of her, only nodded. It was very unlike her to pass up an opportunity to shame Mona over some professional failure. Mona crossed over to the kitchen hesitantly and took a seat opposite her.

"You're . . . out of work early," Mona offered. Rita was wearing her uniform, a pressed white shirt and a medium-length oxblood skirt.

"I had to come home," Rita said dully. It was then that Mona noticed the blood. Rita had shed her stockings and, around one leg like the red stripes of a candy cane, there was a ribbon of red. Mona followed it upward to the chair she was sitting on, a drip of dark blood spilling off the side.

Mona jumped up. "Rita, you're bleeding."

"It's not me," Rita said dully.

"What are you talking about?"

Rita looked desolately at her. This version of her sister, miserable and nonsensical, was the most honest Rita she had seen since they were small children together. "I lost her," Rita said, her voice so small and pained. Mona knelt before her and took her hands, the same way Gene had done days earlier.

"What do you mean, sweetheart?"

"The baby," Rita said absently, as though this were something they had talked of frequently. "I've lost my child." Mona just looked at her, helpless before the wave of feelings moving through her.

It was then that Rita began to sob, crumpling into Mona's arms like a little girl.

· · ·

Rita wasn't sure how far along she had been, two or three months, she thought. She had already decided, though, that the baby was a girl and she was going to name her Katherine and call her Kitty.

Mona helped her clean up and tucked Rita into her bed with towel between her legs and a hot water bladder to hold. She followed the trail of red drips and drabs to the bathroom, where her sister had managed to remove most of the evidence, except for the bloodied towels sitting in the bathtub. Mona scrubbed them out as best she could, the water running pink around her.

After that, she crawled into the bed beside Rita, who was already sleeping deeply, exhausted by her sufferings. The warm, even sensation of her breath, the feeling of her weight on the mattress next to Mona brought something back, something she had not thought of in a very long time. How, when she was little and had nightmares, she would wake up in Rita's arms and Rita wouldn't say anything but would just hold her tighter, like a kind of a reflex.

Mona wrapped her arms now around Rita and kissed the top of her forehead. *It could be like this*, Mona thought, *if it wasn't for Momma and Clark and the pictures.* They could be sisters and take care of one another. Maybe even take care of a baby. *Your cousin Elizabeth will also get with child*, she thought. But Elizabeth had been allowed to keep her child. What any of this meant, Mona could not say.

So she did something else she had not done since she was a child: she prayed. *Dear God*, Mona thought, *tell me what I should do. Give me something, a messenger or a word or something. Anything.*

* * *

When Clark came home, he dragged Mona out of the bed by the crook of her arm. She woke up already halfway to the floor and struggled against him. When she got to her feet, she gave him a slap across the face. Who did he think he was, laying rough hands on her in the very own home?

"Get out of there!" He bellowed. The sound finally woke Rita who rolled over and blinked sleepily at the two of them. "Go to your own damn bed!"

Mona shot a glance at Rita, who was much more composed now. "Go on," she said to Mona. "Clark is here now."

On her way out, Mona could hear him grumbling to Rita about how "she thinks everything under this roof is hers."

"It is, you son of a bitch," Mona murmured to herself. There was a part of her that thought, despite her sister's clear devastation at the loss, it was for the better that she wasn't carrying that man's child. This was no house for a child.

●　●　●

It might not have been the best solution, but it was an affordable one. Misty, the cocktail waitress at *The Paper Lantern* who had filled in for Mona in the number, said she could get her some pills. "You can take 'em with water but I'd drink gin. That's what my Ma did when she needed her monthlies to start up again, a whole bottle if you can manage it. Make sure you do it somewhere safe and quiet. It takes a day or so for everything to get out. Get someone to watch you and make sure you don't bleed too much."

Mona thought of the tragic little pile of stained towels piled in the bathtub after Rita's miscarriage. "How much is too much?"

"You'd know it if you saw it," Misty said, with a kind of breezy confidence that Mona could not muster for herself.

. . .

The problem now was one of timing. This picture was stretching out endlessly, far longer than she'd expected when she signed on, and even though she was merely an extra, she was constantly getting called back to reshoot even the most minor scenes.

Rumor on set was that this was all coming straight from Gideon Vale who was unhappy with nearly every aspect of the production. Allegedly, he was doing extensive rewrites on the script himself and fighting tooth and nail to have his changes implemented.

This was merely what had trickled down to Mona, though. In all her weeks of filming, she had never actually seen the star and she wasn't the only one. When he worked, he demanded a very small set, often just the camera operator, the director, and his scene partner (usually Lydia Leighton). Lately, he had even taken to cutting the director (normally jovial Hapwell Lee) out entirely. People were starting to get worried that the film was going to be shelved, or worse—run out of money.

Mona hadn't gotten all her regular pay yet and she hadn't been paid at all for the weeks beyond the existing schedule. If the picture really did collapse under its own weight, she'd be in even bigger money trouble than she had been before.

Still, it was a job until it wasn't and, right now, it was the only job Mona had. Even the manager at *The Paper Lantern* had booted her after she vomited on stage during a show. So she showed up and she did her best, even though it was a seemingly inconsequential scene of the extras shooting Lydia's character a gossipy look. Hardly a deep acting challenge and Mona thought they'd put this to bed weeks ago but apparently they hadn't gotten it right. Or at least not right *enough*.

The director gestured for them to run through the scene a fourth time when Mona noticed another, unfamiliar person lingering behind the director, nervously rubbing the side of his thumb against his chin.

He must have been there the whole time but she only just now recognized him. In real life, Gideon Vale was not as tall as she would have imagined and his skin was less smooth, with a few small blemishes around his mouth and some freckles on his cheeks. His hair, too, was less glossy and oilier, as though he had not washed it properly in some time. He was wearing what looked to be his costume, or part of it at least—tweed pants and a white shirt. He wasn't wearing any shoes, just his socks.

He didn't look like a film star now; he looked ordinary. Maybe even a little less than ordinary.

He kept touching the director's shoulder, tapping it repeatedly the way a little boy might when he was trying to get his mother's attention. The director would stiffen, his usually cheerful face dull and grave and then Vale would lean down, putting his mouth up close against the other man's ear. Poor Hapwell Lee looked like he wanted to flinch away but was holding himself in place with great effort.

Eventually, though, Gideon seemed to grow tired of this method of intervention and actually walked onto the scene himself.

"No, no, no, no, no," he kept saying, grinding his hands into his hips. Mona wasn't sure but she thought he might be crying. Some of the other girls looked to Lydia, who was staring at her own hands and not making a peep. "You don't understand. None of you. None of you *feel* it."

Gideon Vale's eyes alighted upon Mona and she was transfixed. She saw it now, that star-power, an intensity that made it impossible to look away from him. His face—his eyes—were so expressive and so mobile, everything he felt was so clear and so . . . vital. Right now, he was looking at her with a strange kind of awe. "But you know, don't you? You know the secret, holy mother."

Hearing that word—that name—applied to her sent a strange, sharp thrill through her. She could feel something like panic tingling in the skin of her face. It was like she'd heard some unexpected noise in the dark or seen something move out of the corner of her eye. She felt an animal urge to run, even as Gideon Vale approached her with his hands out.

Mona was aware without looking that the other girls had left her. Lydia Leighton was still there, still unmoving.

"You have felt the weight," Gideon murmured, drawing close to her. "I know, I can see it in you. I can see the light in you. The others . . . they don't understand. It's not just the picture, it's the *light* and we have to get it right. We have to get it right!"

He knelt before her, like he was praying to her. *And the angel came in unto her, and said, Hail, thou that art highly favoured, the Lord is with thee: blessed art thou among women.*

"You know," he said, inching toward her on his knees. "You've felt it. You're the one, look at you." He slid his arms around Mona's hips. It was such a bizarre gesture, a kind of touching Mona had never experienced before. It wasn't maternal—not familial at all, but it wasn't particularly sexual either. It was desperate—she could feel how he was fisting his hands in the fabric of her costume.

Later, when she left the set, she would discover that his sweating palms had left damp spots on her back.

He pushed his face against the swell of her belly,

against that unmistakable pooch that she tried so hard to hide with foundation garments and careful posture. "You have seen the light," he said, almost as though he weren't talking to Mona but to the thing inside her.

The next thing Mona knew, a man was pulling Gideon back from her. He reached for her, again in that desperate, seeking, childlike way. *Fear not, Mary: for thou hast found favour with God. And, behold, thou shalt conceive in thy womb, and bring forth a son, and shalt call his name Jesus.*

Without thinking, Mona reached out to him as well.

• • •

Alan Greeley was the kind of man that Mona had seen since early childhood. They were on the fringes, not stars, not hangers-on, not writers or directors or craftsman but they always carried themselves as though they were more vital than all those people put together. Alan and men like him worked for the studios, or maybe just for themselves, but their jobs, either way, were to smooth out any problems that might arise.

Gideon Vale was apparently such a constant source of these problems that he required Alan to be by his side nearly all the time.

Alan was uncharacteristically alone, however, when he found Mona in wardrobe, smoking a cigarette in the hopes of calming her nerves. She had untucked her white costume shirt and peeled down her shaper to examine her hips where Gideon had grabbed her. Sure enough, there were streaky, finger-shaped red marks there. They would be bruises by morning.

"Mona McKee," Alan said and Mona jumped. Alan seemed to have no reaction to her, half-dressed as she was. Mona grabbed an anonymous robe and threw it on over her unbuttoned shirt and rolled down skirt.

"Yes?" her voice was shaky. So was the cigarette, or rather the hand that held it was.

"Mr. Vale would like to see you in his trailer."

He offered no apologies for Gideon's behavior, no explanation of what exactly had just happened, and no assurances that Mona would be safe if she went alone to a man's trailer. Mona looked around, hoping to see Tiny or at least one of the other women but there was no one. They had given her privacy, taking their smoke break outside.

"I . . . I don't—" Mona began.

"Be just a few minutes of your time," Alan said with cheerful authority. He sounded like an insurance adjustor and it was clear to Mona all of this had already been decided and her agreement was a mere formality.

If her mother were still herself, this would be easily managed. Mona would shrink away and her mother would step forward, full of fury, unstoppable in the face of even the most powerful men-behind-the-men.

Now, though, there was only Mona. Mona, with no money and a looming mortgage payment. Mona, with a shit job as an extra that was blowing up around her. Mona, with an inexplicable baby in her belly.

Mona, who allowed Alan to lead her out to the lot and to Gideon's trailer.

• • •

"Don't worry, Miss," Alan said, in an unexpected moment of compassion as he handed her up the metal staircase leading into the trailer. "Mr. Vale is a good egg. He just wants to talk to you." Alan broke into a broad grin. "Heck, maybe he wants you for a part."

Or he wants you for your parts, said a voice in her head that sounded astonishingly like Rita.

The trailer was nicer than the one that Melody Burke had back when they worked on the *Little Sally* pictures. That was the only other time that Mona had been in a star's accommodations.

Melody's trailer had been . . . different, though. And not just because Melody was a little girl and Gideon a grown man. Melody would not have laid out empty liquor bottles around the built-in bed, nor would she have put a long string of little metal bells and sawed-off tin cans in every doorway. She would not have hammered boards awkwardly over all the windows either.

Vale had been waiting for her. Well, waiting at least. There was a small, formica-topped table folded out and Gideon Vale was sitting hunched in a booth next to it. His elbows were balanced upon the table and he cradled his head in his arms tragically.

"The extra," he mumbled when she stepped into the trailer. He was wearing a night shirt and . . . no pants at all. His feet were completely bare now and, as Mona watched, he flexed and cracked the knuckles in his toes.

"Mr. Vale . . . " Mona fidgeted with her hands.

She wished she had something, even just a purse or a hat, some object to hold between the two of them.

"I knew it was you." Vale turned his face up toward her and he was so pale. It seemed almost as though a light was shining from his skin. "I have been given the burden of the truest sight." He looked pointedly at the seat across the table from him. Mona swallowed hard and approached, stepping through the perimeter of bottles carefully.

He reached out and grabbed her arm in a painful clench. "Shoes," he said and Mona obliged him, slipping her heels off and letting them fall.

Gideon seemed to relax when she sat down, giving a little sigh of relief. "They're watching us very closely now. I'm sorry. I have to take precautions."

Mona wondered if she meant the studio or Alan but she couldn't imagine how taking her shoes off would have anything to do with Alan hearing their conversation.

Gideon moved very quickly, darting his hands across the table to capture her own. "Mama," he said, "you must be vigilant. You have to guard your mind because they can see, if you're not careful, they can see."

"I don't think I understand . . ."

"Inside here." He reached out suddenly and gave her a hard tap in the space between her eyes. Mona reared back automatically but Vale barely seemed to notice. "They'll come in, with the needle, right there. If you aren't so, so careful, Mama."

"D-don't call me that," Mona stammered, trying to pull away from him. He was strong, though, and he pulled back, dragging her inches out of her seat and over the table toward him. "I'm not that."

"You're the vessel," Gideon said, as though he hadn't heard her at all. "They'll cut it out if they find it, remember that."

Mona was off the seat now, stretched painfully across the table and Gideon's face was very close to hers. "You have It," he said, smiling horribly. "It Girl. Have they already told you that? Yes? Yes, I suppose they would have."

Mona was trembling from the effort of trying to keep from falling face-first into him and from fear as well. Gideon Vale was a lunatic and he could hurt her—he could kill her—and no one would save her. They would all stand around and pretend they couldn't hear her screams.

"Alright now," Alan's voice came from the open door as if to contradict Mona's racing thoughts. "That's enough, Gideon."

Vale didn't move, he just kept staring.

"Gideon . . . " Alan said again, warningly.

Vale gave her one last tug, pulling her forward until her head met his mouth in a crash that must have hurt him, though he didn't cry out. She could feel his lips moving against her skin. A kiss? Words? Both? He murmured something. It sounded like, "Be careful, Holy Mother."

• • •

He was harmless, that's what Alan said. Totally

cuckoo but wouldn't hurt a fly. He got a little fix-
ated sometimes on girls—especially pretty ones,
Alan had added with what he probably thought was
a friendly leer. But he never caused any real damage.

Mona thought that the bruises on her hips and
now on her forearms might beg to differ.

What hurt the most, though, was that brief
moment when she had imagined that Gideon Vale
might have seen some sort of truth about her. That
he might be part of . . . some divine plan. She'd
even written it down in her little daybook along
with Misty's instructions for the pills. It was what
she thought of as her list of solutions and it was getting shorter every day. Because Vale wasn't divine,
he was crazy. Only a crazy person could ever believe
that a virgin could get with child.

She was starting to cry, halfway across the lot,
when Gene caught up with her. It had been more
than an hour now since the director sent everyone home; he must have been waiting on her. He

touched her arm and as soon as she looked at his wondering face, the tears began to flow in earnest.

"Mona, Mona, Mona," he wrapped his arms around her, rocked her against him like an upset child. "What happened, Mona?"

"I thought . . ." Mona managed, but that was all. What had she thought? That God smiled upon bit players in Hollywood? That her womb was blessed? That she had a destiny beyond trying to abort her pregnancy with a hope and a pill and a bottle of gin?

Gene shushed her, wiping the tears from her face with his fingers. "It's all going to come out fine," he said. "You'll come stay at my place and we'll sort this all out, okay?"

Gene's place. Far from home, quiet and safe. The pills in her pocket seemed to have taken on a special, inordinate weight and it seemed that now, finally, was the time to use them.

"Alright," she said, "let me get some things together. And write a note for my sister."

9

Final Girl

"**W**ell," said Flavia when I showed her the footage of Vale and Mona, "that's fucked up. And thanks for waking me, by the way."

"I'm showing you now," I protested. "And that's not the point anyway. Do you think he could be the Baby Daddy?"

"I think he's unhinged," Flavia snorted. "But, yeah, I mean it's certainly possible, right? Though wasn't Gideon Vale supposed to be infertile?"

"It's been speculated," I admitted. There was no real way of proving it at this point but it was true that Vale never fathered any known children despite spending almost two decades in a committed relationship and engaging in numerous other sexual affairs. Maybe he was just really great at the rhythm method?

I looked down at the opened suitcase. A pink pair of cropped pants, an ordinary white shirt, a pair of white socks, all neatly folded like they were just waiting for their owner to pick them up again. "I was really hoping that Mona's last diary would be in there," I mused. "Though, I suppose you can't have everything."

Flavia picked a ravel on the hotel comforter, an uncharacteristically quiet response. "That last diary . . . do you have any idea what it might look like?"

"Do you mean like physically? She typically used regular notebooks, so it probably wouldn't look like much of anything."

"No, I meant the writing. Would it be, like, normal writing or . . . different?"

I looked at her and she was still picking at that

damned comforter. "Flavia," I said slowly, "have you seen Mona's diary?"

She sighed. "I don't know. I have this . . . book. It came in a package when I ordered this anniversary bundle of *Little Sally* movies."

I remembered that bundle! I'd bid on it when it came to auction, even though I had copies of all the films included. *Flavia* was the one who outbid me?

"The person who sold it to me said they got it at an estate sale in San Luis Obispo and the films and the book were together then. He didn't know what to make of it but figured they were related. I can't read it, so I don't know anything for sure . . ."

"And you were just going to keep that under your hat?"

"I didn't even know that Mona kept diaries," Flavia protested. "Not until you mentioned it."

"If you had read my blog—"

"Your blog is dull, pedantic, and self-righteous. No one reads that shit!"

"But you brought it, right? The diary?"

"I brought scans," she said witheringly. "Like I'm going to bring a primary source across the country to a convention."

Well, she did have a little bit of the scholar in her, I guessed. "Show me," I said, gesturing toward her phone. "I know Mona's code."

Flavia grinned, seemingly in spite of herself. "Seriously? I've been working on this for three months."

"Once again, if you had read my blog . . ."

* * *

Flavia's scans were pretty good quality, though obviously it was slow going working from a tiny cell phone screen. I set up on the room's complimentary desk and began the painstaking process of going through the document line by line.

Good thing I had memorized Mona's substitution cipher.

It didn't appear to be the entire six-month diary,

unless Mona suddenly got a lot less verbose and, strangely, the handwriting was off. Almost all of Mona's diaries were writing in small, neat block printing while this was in a more flowing feminine hand.

But it was definitely Mona's code, no doubt about that.

The first line was the date—February 1st—just a few days before Mona disappeared, and the first line of text was ominous: "I have come to believe that I am dying."

• • •

I know the signs of dying, I have been watching Mother after all. Every morning, I wake sick and slow, my head aching, my limbs sore. I'm so tired. I'm on the thinnest ice at work, missed two days last week because I couldn't wake up when the alarm went.

I have the same thing that she had. It's why I vomit and why my hair comes out so easily and it's why my baby couldn't stay inside of me. I am poisoned and I know from looking after Mother that it will only get worse. I will get weaker and weaker until I can't feed myself or even hobble to the toilet.

It will be easier then for you to manage, with the both of us gone. That's what we've been preparing you for all along: a life focused solely on yourself. I'm writing this for you, though. I want you to find it after I'm dead so that at least then you will know everything we did for you.

Without us, there would be no Mona McKee.

* * *

I paused in my transcription and stared down at the words I'd written on the complimentary hotel notepad. "This isn't Mona's diary," I told Flavia, who was watching more of *The Redfield House.*

"But you said it was her code?"

"It is but . . . I think her sister Rita wrote this."

"Whoa!" Flavia sprung off the bed. "Why would Rita be writing in Mona's code?"

I looked again at the paragraph I'd transcribed, the resignation and the bitterness in it. "Because she intended it for Mona's eyes."

Flavia scanned the paragraph, a look of slow-growing confusion on her face. "What's she talking about with this dying thing? She outlived Mona, that's for sure."

"There's only one way to find out," I said, scrolling down to the next un-translated paragraph.

I remember the first time I knew something was beautiful. I was young, too young to really understand what it meant, feeling that way about another person. She was my own age and we were running around playing chase on a playground. She hooked her legs over the metal monkey bars and allowed her body to hang down, brown curls falling all in her face. She laughed and brushed them away and the sun caught her hair, gleamed in it. That was beautiful. She was beautiful.

Mother knew, of course. She knew before anyone else and she said it was all for the best. That way, she could keep having me do the things she wanted me to do with the men who made your career and, like she told me, "there wouldn't be any feelings" because I wasn't that way.

"It won't cost you much to give away something you weren't ever going to use," she said to me.

It was me, Mona, who did what you wouldn't do. What Mother wouldn't ever let you do and what she couldn't do herself. You were her money in the bank and I was her spending cash.

Didn't you ever wonder why I had nightmares? Why we had to stop sleeping in the same bed because I would wet? Didn't it seem strange to you when we were nine and got the chicken pox how hard I scratched at them, how deep I dug?

Mother taped oven mitts to your hands and watched over you with a wooden spoon, ready to paddle you red if you so much as rubbed a spot but I was allowed to make pits—scars—all over me?

Did you really not know?

It didn't even work, the scars. Because those men never cared about my face to begin with.

The only thing that worked was time, the great cure. They didn't have any interest in women and the ones who did weren't interested in me. Mother washed her hands of me then but I didn't care because I thought I was finally free. You'd made it to the top and Mother had no more use for me. I could go out and be a mother.

That was all I ever wanted to do. The only thing I figured I'd be really good at—I knew exactly what not to do.

You need a man for that like you do for most things and I found out that even the regular men didn't want nothing to do with me. Mother told me once that they could smell it on me, my unnaturalness, and that drove them off.

And then I met Clark. Like Mother, he knew without me telling him but he liked that about me. I never liked being with him in the way that husbands and wives are (just like I had never liked it with any menfolk) but Clark loved me not liking it. Clark loved me entirely.

You can't understand that because everyone loves you. You will have a million chances for a family but Clark is probably my only shot. Who else would tolerate what I am? Who else would want me to be a mother to their children?

I was so proud when I brought him home, so happy about my good luck and I'll never forget how you looked at me that night. You pitied me. The best thing I could have hoped for and you pitied me.

And now I'm going to die, all without ever getting anything more than the scraps and leftovers, the worst version of what you have always taken for granted. I hope that when we are dead you will finally understand how much of us went into you. Maybe then, finally, you will be capable of gratitude.

February 2nd, 1953

You didn't come home tonight. I sent Clark out after you, first to the lot and then on aimless drives around the neighborhood. I wonder if, after years of inching yourself away from Mother and me, you have finally decided to run?

February 4th, 1953

Mother calls for you. She doesn't want anyone else to feed her. Clark gets angry because she resists and flails and gets food all over her bedding. He says she is difficult and I think of how he would have managed with her as she was before. He wouldn't, of course. Mother never would have let me marry Clark.

She never would have let you get away either.

February 10th, 1953

Your friend came to the house today. I didn't know you had any friends like that. Funny, all these years in Hollywood and she is the closest thing to a star I've ever seen. I've always imagined a star was someone who was a little brighter, a little more solid and shining than the rest of the world.

She was asking after you, wondering if we'd had any word. I told her that we hadn't and that I figured you had gotten tired of this place. Of us.

Clark came home while she was there. He had been drinking, I could tell and he was angry, as usual.

It was just like that night we went to see your

show. Do you remember that? Do you remember the little waitress who danced with you? Clark thought I paid her too much attention and he thought the same about your little friend. That's the worst thing he could imagine, his wife throwing him over for a woman.

He doesn't understand that I wouldn't ever do anything with those girls, not even if I wanted to. Why in the world would girls like them have someone like me?

February 13th, 1953

Clark and I fought again, a real doozy this time. I was upset anyway because I'd been almost a week late but then Aunt Flo came knocking. Clark was still mad about your friend coming around and he's been getting worse and worse the longer he goes without work. I thought he broke my arm at first but now I can tell it's just sore. I'm better this morning, not feeling sick, even. No headache.

Mother is worse, however. It's like the two of us are on a see-saw, one can never be up without the other one sinking down. She calls out for you at night and wakes Clark up. Once, she even mistook me for you. She touched my hair and called me "beautiful girl."

February 23rd, 1953

Your beautiful little friend is dead, Mona. Someone killed her horribly in her own apartment. I read all about it in the paper, they even ran some pictures of her apartment. None of her, thank God, but it looks like the criminal made free with everything she had.

The papers say she never fought. It's like she slept through the entire thing and I don't know how that can be possible.

March 1st, 1953

Clark finally got a job. It's just a factory job and he's working third shift, coming home around three in the morning but it's something. Maybe now things will get a little bit easier. Mother is getting worse and fast. I called the doctor and described everything that is happening to her and he says it won't be long now.

That, too, will make things easier.

March 18th, 1953

Mother died today. Well, sometime in the night. When I got up this morning to make her breakfast she was lying there with her mouth open. She wouldn't have liked that, looking ridiculous. I couldn't make her mouth stay closed (could we ever?) so I pulled a blanket up over her.

We will have to have a funeral now and Clark will be no help at all. I wish you were here, Mona. We are a month behind on the mortgage and I don't see how we're going to pay this month's bill either, let alone an undertaker. That was supposed to be the deal, Mona: this family formed around you, lifted you up and gave you the first and best of everything and, in exchange, you would take care of us.

You didn't keep your end of the bargain.

March 26th, 1953

It took me a minute to recognize her face when I saw it in the newspaper today. I knew that I remembered her from somewhere but it's been a few months since I saw her. When I read her name, I knew. "Misty." An unusual name.

The police won't say anything but they think that the one that killed Tiny is the same one that got her. The newspapers said that she didn't fight either which surprised me. She looked like a fighter.

We buried Momma down in Long Beach, which I think she would have liked. It cost too much to send her upstate to be with her people. Maybe someday we'll put a marker there for you.

Because you didn't run away, did you, Mona?

April 9th, 1953

I found your diary. You were never very good at keeping it hidden and I don't understand why you bothered. We shared a womb for nine months, what could you possibly keep from me?

You could keep from me the contents of your own womb, I suppose.

I would have helped you, Mona. How could you not know that? I would have raised your baby as though it were my own. We would have been a family.

I would have been a mother.

Instead, we have nothing.

"Wait, that's it?" Flavia grabbed the notebook from me like I might be hiding something underneath it. "That's all she wrote?"

"That's all that's in the scans you gave me."

"Well, that's everything I have," she said, defeated. "It just . . . seems like there should be more."

I knew what she meant. Or rather, I knew what she wanted: she wanted the parlor scene. She wanted the detective or the PI to stare down the murderer explain how he did it. She wanted the clever solution and the satisfying ending.

She was never going to get it, though. I'd known that once but I'd allowed myself to get distracted by the driving buzz of discovery. I'd let myself forget for just a second that this was Mona's real life, not one of her films.

At the end of a film, I knew what had happened and I understood why. I was comfortable leaving those characters, certain that their stories were complete. That was the only place in the world I could reliably get that feeling, that surety. I wondered now if that was part of what had drawn Mona to pictures herself. On the screen, she could encapsulate a whole life with none of the messiness, the unanswered questions and unaddressed resentments of her real existence. On the screen, she got more than just *an* ending, she got dozens of them.

"Look," I said, "why don't we watch the rest of the *Little Sally* pictures? Those are complete."

Flavia sat down on the edge of the bed and looked thoughtfully at the TV. "Sure," she said, "she would have wanted us to watch."

That, I thought, was true enough. There were many things we couldn't do for poor, lost Mona McKee but there was one thing we could give her, one thing she'd chased all her short life: an audience.

10

Dead Ends

Gene lived in a tall, slender apartment built around a twisting staircase. The kitchen and the living room were downstairs, whereas the guest room he intended for Mona to use was upstairs. Gene's wife Suzanne was away, he said, at her mother's for the weekend but their little daughter was dozing in a crib in the living room.

They spoke quietly and moved delicately to avoid waking the child as Gene led her up the stairs to a small bedroom with an adjacent bathroom. Mona was glad of that feature. She had a brief but vivid mental image of lowering herself into the bathtub there and waiting for the blood to come.

"Mona," Gene already sounded uncomfortable, "I wanted to tell you something."

He took her hand gently and led her over to the bed, sitting them both down on its edge. With her other hand, Mona still clutched her suitcase.

"I know," Gene said slowly, "what your difficulty is."

She had supposed something like this, why else would he treat her with kid gloves?

"How long have you known?"

"A few weeks," Gene said. "You're," he gestured at her torso and reddened slightly, "getting bigger."

This only confirmed for Mona that she was making the correct decision. If this was something that Gene could see, soon there would be no hiding it at all.

"I want you to know, though, that I don't think anything less of you. I know you've been in this business for a long time, Mona, but you are still a young woman and many young women have been taken in by a charming older fella's lies."

He meant well, that much was clear, and even though Mona realized that his conclusions made sense for what he knew of her situation, she could not suppress the bloom of fury in her stomach at his words. She was so occupied thinking up a sharp retort that she almost missed what he said next:

"But even if that bastard didn't keep his promises, I will. I'll marry you, Mona."

The room was so silent, Mona imagined she could feel both of their hearts beating.

The strangest thing of all was how not-strange he looked to her. His face was the same, his eyes had no manic glint in them, his cheeks were not flushed with excitement. He was just Gene, making what was, as far as he was concerned, a totally reasonable offer.

"We can figure it out. I'll take care of you and I'll take care of the baby, too." He reached out and pressed the flat of his hand against her stomach. Mona felt frozen, though everything in her wanted to break away from him, crawl away from him if she had to.

"You're already married . . . " she said weakly.

"I don't love her." Gene moved closer to her eagerly, as though he had been waiting to hear those exact words from her. "I've never loved her. It was an accident, just like you had. A stupid mistake. But I do love you." He touched the side of her face, cupping her chin and jaw in his hand.

Mona felt as though she had slipped through some sort of tear in the world and emerged in another place, similar to the life she knew but fundamentally different. Was this really Gene, professing his love for her while his own daughter napped in the next room?

It seemed impossible that he could inch any closer to her, and yet he did. All she could smell was the soap he used and the cream he brushed into his hair. Up close, it was horrible, sending her stomach lurching. All of this seemed terrifyingly familiar, this sensation of encroaching . . . maleness. These smells, the pressure of his hands on her and the damp heat of his breathing.

Most familiar of all, her own inability to move or resist or even to tell him "no," though she had never wanted anything less in her life.

He kissed her, either not noticing or not caring that her mouth was rigid and unresponsive and her body was in the same stiff pose it had been since he first made his overtures.

"Oh, Mona," he said, tangling his fingers in her hair.

Something about his voice seemed to resonate inside of her, breaking up the ice that had kept her motionless. "Stop!" she said fiercely, pushing him back. "You're acting like a crazy person, Gene!"

Gene looked genuinely shocked. Was it possible that he really and truly believed that his feelings were reciprocated? That her confusion and alarm were actually passion and longing? Could he be that stupid or that willfully blind?

When he spoke again, his voice had chilled by

several degrees. "You still think you can do better? How many other offers do you have on the table, Mona?" It was cruel, what he was saying, but Mona almost preferred it to his overheated tones earlier. There was something unavoidably honest about it. This was what Gene thought of her: an uppity girl who thought too highly of herself. Well, she thought highly enough of herself not to stay one more minute there with him.

Mona stood up, half-stumbling back to the open door.

"Mona!" Gene cried out, immediately contrite. "Wait! You can still stay!"

Mona hurried down the staircase so fast that she nearly slipped. For a moment, she almost wished she had. Falling down the stairs was, after all, a classic way of resolving her particular problem.

Gene's head appeared in the shadow of the open bedroom door above her. "Mona," he pleaded and she looked up at him, hopeful against all reason that he was going to apologize, say he'd had a fit of insanity and go back to being her friend. Instead, he almost whimpered as he said, "Please don't hate me. I couldn't stand it if you hated me."

Mona was halfway home before she even remembered that she'd left her suitcase in Gene's guest bedroom.

* * *

She could still feel the quiver in her legs when she got home and she must have looked pretty shaken up because even Clark, hardly the most sensitive and observant of men, noticed.

"What's wrong with you?" He asked, sitting at the kitchen table with a peanut butter sandwich in front of him. Momma was sleeping deeply in the bed in the front room. There was no sign of Rita, which made sense for the mid-afternoon.

Mona made her way to the table unsteadily. What was wrong with her? The answer was so lengthy and so complicated that, instead, she simply took the other half of Clark's sandwich and commenced to eating it.

Clark watched her do it with uncharacteristic calm, his eyes dark and thoughtful on her.

"I'm pregnant," Mona said, between bites. It felt strangely good to say that aloud, here in her own kitchen. Though she did look over her shoulder at the sofa bed to make sure that her mother was still sleeping. "And I don't know how I got that way but I have to deal with it all the same."

There was a kind of slow-creeping horror on Clark's face and Mona was perversely glad to see it. It hardly seemed fair that she should be the only one to bear all of this distress and fear.

"Have you told Rita?" Clark asked her, his voice just a smoky rasp.

The irony of him asking her that question in the very chair where Rita had sat, bleeding from her lost child, did not escape Mona. "I can't," she said.

"No," Clark agreed immediately. "You can't."

He stood up, pushing the chair back from the

table with his body. "We've got to . . . figure this out . . ." He ran his hand through his hair, creating greasy furrows.

"We?" Mona asked, cocking her head at him.

"How much does it cost? To get it taken care of? We can get the money."

It occurred to Mona that, not so long ago, she would have been delighted to hear one of her family members say something like that. Now, though, she felt a strong sense of discomfort. Clark's reaction to this information was extreme, even for a man with such a fragile temperament.

"I can pay my own way," Mona told him. "Just like I do with everything else."

Clark turned to look at her and his expression was so bitter that Mona wondered if he was going to take a swing at her. He never had before and Mona didn't know if it was Rita's intercession or out of respect for the fact that Mona legally owned the home he occupied. If he did, Mona was ready for him. A part of her had been expecting it since she saw the first finger-shaped bruises on her sister's arms.

"I thought you couldn't have a baby . . . like her."

Mona could feel her own face twisting into an incredulous sneer. "Why the hell would you think that?"

"Because I've been fucking you for the better part of a year!" Clark shouted and Mona reflexively looked over her shoulder at the sofa bed where her mother slept on, seemingly untroubled. "And now—now!—you get knocked up! Right when your sister is tying herself into knots with wanting a baby. This is gonna kill her."

Mona stared at her mother. Suddenly, it seemed that was all she could focus on—that absence, that stillness, that awful silence. Her mother should be awake. Her mother would not sleep through this. Her mother would not let this happen to her.

Mona rose from her chair and went to her mother's bedside. She touched the old woman's wrist and her throat, felt a steady but languid pulse of blood there. Her eyes were closed, the lids shot through with blue veins and they did not even flutter at Mona's touch.

"What's wrong with her?" Mona demanded of Clark, who had sat back down, covering the back of his head with his hands. "What did you do to her?"

"She's fine," Clark said, without lifting his head.

"Is she dying?"

"She's got a tumor in her brain, of course she's dying."

Mona rose up again, moving toward the telephone affixed to the kitchen wall. Clark moved to intercept her with surprising speed, grabbing her outstretched hand and bending it back painfully.

"What did you do to her?" Mona cried out, trying desperately not to show how much his grip on her hand hurt.

"Nothing I haven't done before." He pulled her over to the table again. "Give her a little peace and me a little quiet."

"What are you talking about?" Mona writhed in

his grip and crushed her hands until sharp bolts of pain shot up her forearm.

Clark shoved her down into a kitchen chair and crouched down before her, grabbing her other hand so that both of them were in his control. It looked absurdly like some sort of romantic scene, a suitor kneeling before his beloved. Her hands throbbed painfully in his inescapable grasp.

"We're going to keep this quiet," Clark said soothingly and Mona didn't know who he was trying to comfort. Probably himself. "We're gonna get that baby out of you and then . . . then we're gonna get you fixed so this never happens again. And Rita's not gonna hear anything about it."

Mona just stared at him. What was there to say in the face of such utter insanity?

"Say it," Clark demanded. "Say that Rita won't ever find out."

Mona's mouth felt creaky, like old machinery that hadn't been looked after. "Rita . . . Rita won't ever find out . . . " she stammered.

Clark looked at her with genuine disappointment on his face. "No," he said softly. "That's not gonna work, is it?"

Mona's last clear thought before he began to hit her was, *Guess I'm not such a good actress after all.*

· · ·

The manager at the grocery store sent them all home early. Another girl got killed and the rumor was, it was Soledad. Soledad, with the deep dimples and big, pregnant belly that Rita tried not to stare enviously at. Maybe someone followed her home from a late shift at the store. Maybe the manager didn't want to take that risk.

Maybe Rita was a bad luck charm. What else would you call when people around a person started dropping like flies? Mona, Mona's friend, that pretty waitress, and now a girl from work; what could that be but a curse?

The house was empty when Rita got there; Clark

wasn't even sleeping in the bedroom. Rita had long suspected that he actually went out drinking during the day while she was at work and she supposed this was proof. He'd be gone all night as well, working an assembly line job and Rita would be alone.

It was an unusual sensation, loneliness. For most of her life. Rita felt overwhelmed by the presence of others. To be a twin was to always be in company, after all. From the very moment of her birth. She was learning now, at nineteen years old, how to manage with just herself.

She considered lying down for a nap—she never slept well—but a telephone call interrupted her. The voice on the other end was unfamiliar. It was a man, slightly raspy sounding with a queer accent she couldn't exactly place. It was almost . . . western? But not quite.

"Are you Miss Mona McKee's next of kin?"

"I'm her sister, if that's what you mean," Rita said warily. She'd fielded more than a few calls from real weirdos after Mona's purse was found in the park.

The police officer working Mona's case suggested that she change her phone number but Rita figured that, with the way the bills were piling up, she wouldn't have to worry about it much longer.

"You and me, we got something in common then."

"How so?"

"My name is JJ Malliski. My sister was killed a few months ago."

"Yeah," Rita said, "I read about that." *Woman Dismembered in Bloody House of Horrors!* the papers had said with all their characteristic sensitivity.

"I think the person who killed her killed your sister too."

"Who said my sister's dead?" Everyone did, though. They said it without saying it, by the pity in their eyes and the way they spoke about her: hushed and always in the past-tense.

"Listen, did the police ever say anything to you about a Dr. Winston? Did Mona ever mention him?"

She had, though not to Rita herself. She'd

confided in her diary about Dr. Winston, how he'd humiliated and dismissed her and left her hanging out to dry. As angry—as betrayed—as Rita felt at the idea of her sister purging a perfectly healthy baby from her body, she'd been angry too at the doctor's behavior. Her sister was a good girl, nice and clean and straight as an arrow. What had it all been for? Rita's lost innocence and their mother's endless machinations, if Mona wasn't able to hang on to that purity.

"She mentioned a doctor," Rita told him. "She was having stomach troubles." Rita was hesitant to get into the details of Mona's condition. For all she knew, this man could be a particularly unscrupulous reporter trying to sniff out a lead.

"Yeah, I'll bet. Probably the same stomach troubles my sister had." The man sighed into the phone. "I'm not interested in telling secrets, the good lord knows I got enough of my own. I just got a bad feeling about this doctor. Did you know they found something in my sister's blood? Some kind of sedative."

So that was why she didn't fight back, she'd been

too drugged up to move, probably. How horrifying that must have been, knowing someone was creeping toward you, meaning you such terrible harm, and not being able to move or even to scream? Rita squeezed her eyes closed and gave a shuddering breath.

"But why would he kill her like that? Like . . . like some maniac?"

"Maybe he thought she was gonna expose him?" JJ offered. "My sister wasn't no angel, but I've never known anyone else to love so fiercely as she did. If she decided you were one of the people who meant something to her, there was nothing she wouldn't do for you." His voice had warmed and become less rasping. "If she thought Winston had something to do with Mona going missing, she would have sussed it out. Even if it killed her."

There was at least some truth to what he was saying. Tiny had come around to the house, asked about Mona and where she might be. She was the only one, in fact, who had visited. More than a decade in showbiz and none of those big, marquee names even knew Mona was alive. Or not alive.

"But what about the other ones?" Rita pointed out. Dr. Winston would have no need to silence a cocktail waitress and a grocery store clerk and why would anyone commit four murders to cover up one accidental death?

"I don't know," JJ admitted. "I just have a feeling that they're connected somehow. The way he—" JJ's voice grew thick for the first time as though he were resisting against some sort of surprise swell of emotion. "The way he cut on her, the sedation, it just seems like something a doctor might do."

"Was it the sort of sedative he used? Maybe you can get the police to check his office for it?"

"No. It was actually . . . hold on a minute, I wrote it down." JJ paused and Rita could hear the rustling of papers on the other end of the line. "Yeah. It was an animal sedative, I guess. Mostly used on cattle."

"Cattle?" Rita repeated helplessly. She felt suddenly as though she were floating inside herself, as though a small core of her . . . soul? . . . had gotten loose and was drifting inside her too-large body. A cattle sedative, the kind that Clark would have ready access to at the dairy farm. Clark, who hated Mona, who erupted into a rage when Rita so much as glanced sideways at another woman. Like a pretty waitress, or a coworker, or an unfamiliar visitor.

"Yeah, they don't know too much about it, but it's pretty common in California."

"And what . . . what would she have felt? When he gave her the sedative? What are the . . . the symptoms?"

JJ rustled more paper. "I'm not too sure on that. It's not intended for humans, so I don't think they really know much about what it would do to them."

It would give them headaches, Rita realized. It would make them nauseous and overtired. It would put them into a sleep so deep that someone could do just about anything to them. And then, finally, it would make them forget.

"Why do you ask? Do you know something about this?"

"No," Rita said automatically. "I don't know anything."

. . .

When Clark brought home the little handgun, he told her that it was for protection. "There's crazies out there," he said, touching her face.

Rita retrieved it from its place beneath the bed and went to the kitchen table where she scrupulously cleaned the weapon and loaded it. She left all the paraphernalia out on the table as neatly arrayed as any tea service.

She sat then in what had been her mother's favorite chair and waited. Sooner or later, her husband would come home and then she would do exactly what he'd asked her to: she would make her house safe.

AUTHOR'S NOTE

*J*ean Spangler, 26, brunette, can dance a bit. Has a Vivien Leigh-meets-Elizabeth Short look.

A casting director in 1949 might have described Jean that way, if he described her at all. Jean was a very minor star in the firmament of '40s Hollywood. More of a meteor, really.

She had taken a winding road to pictures, starting out as a dancer in her teens but getting sidetracked by a disastrous marriage. After her divorce in 1946, Jean took up dancing again to pay the bills and that led to some minor roles in a few films.

By all accounts, Jean loved performing and she

was glad to have a career that allowed her to provide not just for herself and her daughter but also for her mother, brother, and sister-in-law. In fact, the only cloud on Jean's horizon appeared to be her ex, Dexter Benner, with whom she was engaged in a protracted custody battle over the pair's daughter Christine.

Benner claimed that Jean was a "glamor girl" who cared more about partying than being a mom while Jean alleged that Dexter was abusive during their marriage and afterward. After a grueling two-year long court battle, Jean was finally awarded primary custody with the judge definitively stating that her occupation as an entertainer did not preclude her from being a good caregiver for her child.

Dexter Benner was not the only bad relationship in Jean's past—or her present. He wasn't the only man to hit her or threaten her life and she had been linked by various sources to men with reputations for brutality.

It was the men in Jean's life who became the

focus of the story in October of 1949—mainly because it seemed likely that one of them had murdered her.

Creating a timeline of Jean's movements on the last day she was known to be alive—October 7th, 1949—is a challenge. When she left the house that day, seemingly casually, she told her sister-in-law that she was going to meet with Benner in regard to some overdue child support he owed her. Benner would later dispute this, saying he had no plans to see her that day and, indeed, had not seen her in weeks. His new wife backed up his story.

Jean had also explained that she was going to be out late because she had a night shoot. When she called the house at seven to check on Christine, she confirmed this, advising her sister not to wait up. Investigators would later discover that Jean was not scheduled to work on any films at that time.

The sightings of Jean after she left her house vary in terms of reliability but a store owner who claimed to have seen her milling around a farmer's market near her home for about an hour and a half at six p.m. is generally treated as credible. The store owner said Jean appeared to be waiting for someone.

Several other witnesses placed her at a local bar called *The Cheesebox* at various points in the evening of the seventh and early morning of the eighth. The accuracy of these sightings is debated. After that, things get a little . . . weird. Subsequent sightings mainly involve one individual—often someone who did not personally know Jean—claiming to have seen her in various improbable locations: a convertible headed out of town, a bar in Fresno, a drive-in restaurant in Monterey, a hotel in El Paso.

What is known for sure is Jean did not come home that night, nor would she ever come home again. At some point, someone dumped her purse (the strap torn but the contents apparently intact) in Griffith Park, likely in a small window of time on October 8th.

It was that purse—or rather, what was inside it—that would turn this from a standard missing person's case to an enduring Tinseltown mystery. Inside the purse was an unfinished note that Jean had addressed to someone named "Kirk," It read, *Can't wait any longer, Going to see Dr. Scott. It will work best this way while mother is away,*

Note the comma, which suggests that the note was unfinished.

Predictably, this ignited an orgy of gossip. The rumor was that Jean was three months pregnant when she died and that "Dr. Scott" was an abortionist. There was allegedly a medical student known to provide terminations under the table but investigators were never able to substantiate this, nor were they able to find any relevant doctors with a name like Scott.

The second, related rumor was that the Kirk of the note was rising star Kirk Douglas, who had in fact worked with Jean very recently on a film called *Young Man With a Horn*. Douglas was not yet the megastar he would become in the 1950s and '60s, but he was considered to be a promising up-and-comer. A friend of Jean's told investigators that that Jean had claimed she would soon be coming into a lot of money and many began speculating that Jean had been pregnant and was blackmailing the then-married Douglas.

Kirk Douglas apparently caught wind of these rumors—or anticipated them—and called investigators directly just days after the purse was located. He wanted to note for the record that he had worked on a movie with Jean but the two had never met personally and he was not the Kirk she'd addressed.

This move probably wound up raising a lot of the eyebrows it intended to settle but, in the end, police never found any real links to Kirk Douglas. Though Jean was alleged to have dated several men, Douglas was not known to be one of them (her mother did claim that she'd gone out with someone named Kirk on a couple of occasions, but she'd never met or even seen the man). Furthermore, he was in Palm Springs when she vanished. Additionally, one has to imagine that if the goal was to prevent Jean from exposing her connection to Douglas, a note that linked the two of them would be the first thing any abductor destroyed.

The sightings of Jean further afield in California gave rise to the next most popular theory: the mob connection. Jean had apparently dated Davy Ogul, an alleged enforcer for Mickey Cohen, king of the crime scene in 1940s LA. When Ogul himself disappeared just two days after Jean, it seemed too perfect to be a coincidence. Had Jean gotten involved somehow in mob dealings? Had she been forced to go on the run—or be eliminated—along with Ogul?

Again, investigators could never actually find any real evidence to support this.

The next common theory arose with the benefit of hindsight: perhaps Jean had run afoul of a serial killer?

It wasn't completely out of left field—there were a number of high profile crimes against young women in LA at that time, specifically the brutal murder of Elizabeth Short (who was destined to be forever known by what had only been a casual nickname: The Black Dahlia) and the strange home-invasion and murder of wealthy heiress Georgette Bauerdorf in her own apartment. As the years went on and Jean's case cooled, people began to speculate that her disappearance could be related to some of these other murders.

This theory, too, can't really be verified in any meaningful way. Neither Elizabeth Short nor Georgette Bauerdorf's murders were ever solved (nor were they ever linked in anything other than speculation) and Jean was never found. It is not impossible that all of these crimes were the doing of one individual but there's no specific reason to believe that and several to doubt it.

The crimes were similar but hardly identical and the victims themselves led very different lives and occupied different socio-economic stations. Additionally, when you examine that list, Jean stands out by her very absence—her body was never found whereas Elizabeth's and, to a lesser extent,

Georgette's, were put on display. Whoever murdered Elizabeth Short wanted her found and the person who killed Georgette Bauerdorf at the very least didn't care much if her body was discovered. Whoever took Jean also apparently took steps to conceal what happened to her, including dumping her purse at a location that was almost certainly not the abduction site.

In death, Jean has acquired a notoriety that she never really achieved in life. The girl who went uncredited in most of her films has attained mythic status in real life. The theories about how and why she vanished are, well, the stuff of Hollywood films. There is one other possibility, however, that is tragically mundane. In fact, it happens to more than 1,000 women each year in the US.

Dexter Benner was a natural person of interest when Jean disappeared. He was alleged to have physically abused her in the past, threatening her on multiple occasions, including once telling her he'd "fix it so [she'd] never see [her] kid again." He had just come off a contentious custody battle that had not gone in his favor and Jean's statement to her sister suggested that she was going to meet him on the day she vanished. If that statement was true—or even partially true—he may have also owed Jean back child support

October 7th was the day before Benner was scheduled to take Christine for his custodial weekend and he did indeed pick up his daughter and, just as he had done many times in the past, he refused to bring her back when his time was up. He even wound up serving two weeks in jail for contempt of court because he refused to let Jean's mother see her granddaughter. Almost as soon as Benner was released from jail, he took Christine and his second wife and headed for Florida, never to return. Jean's family never saw Christine again.

Of all the proposed suspects, Dexter Benner perhaps benefitted the most from Jean's disappearance. With her gone, it was much easier to take full custody of Christine by force, something he did less than forty-eight hours after Jean vanished. According to Jean herself, Benner had been violent towards her in the past, particularly when she resisted his efforts to control her, either by leaving or by attempting to enforce their custody agreement.

Dexter Benner's alibi was supplied by his second wife, to whom he had been married for just one month at that time.

None of this proves that Benner in any way harmed his ex-wife but, in my personal opinion, this has always been the most reasonable scenario. Jean and Dexter's interactions fit very neatly into a pattern common to abusers and those they abuse. The threats, the continual disregard for the authority of the court and the legitimacy of the custody agreement, the lashing back at Jean's "lifestyle," all of those moves could be straight from The Abusive Partner's Handbook.

Statistically, if a woman is going to be murdered in United States, it will be at the hands of a former or current partner. Sixty-three percent of female homicides fit this description. Statistics and case studies also tell us that the most dangerous moments for these women are when they are somehow challenging the abusive partner's control over them. That is why the leading cause of death for a pregnant woman is homicide and that is why the period of time when a person leaves their abuser is the most physically dangerous.

When a certain kind of person feels that their grip over another human is being challenged, they lash out violently. A changed custody agreement would definitely qualify as a challenge to an abuser's authority over both the former partner and the child, whom abusers often regard as more object than person—a thing that rightfully belongs to them. It is common for an abusive partner to tell his victim that he will kill her if she leaves him and it is equally common for him to do just that. Two-thirds of all intimate partner homicides take place after the relationship has ended.

These sorts of crime are "normal" in the purest

sense of the world. Common, standard, quite literally "everyday." Some estimates say as many as three women per day are murdered by current or former partners. In some ways, it is almost comforting to imagine that Jean was swept up in something big and bizarre and operatic, that she became the enigmatic McGuffin in a hard-boiled Hollywood mystery. It is disheartening to think that her death was not at all mysterious and that, if we really knew all the details of her fate, people would have forgotten her long ago. After all, what is one more domestic gone wrong? What is one more name in that unending bloody roster?